Manson and Woods Christie

Collection of Armour and Arms

Carvings in Ivory

Manson and Woods Christie

Collection of Armour and Arms
Carvings in Ivory

ISBN/EAN: 9783742819802

Manufactured in Europe, USA, Canada, Australia, Japa

Cover: Foto ©Andreas Hilbeck / pixelio.de

Manufactured and distributed by brebook publishing software
(www.brebook.com)

Manson and Woods Christie

Collection of Armour and Arms

CATALOGUE

OF THE

VALUABLE AND EXTENSIVE COLLECTION OF

ARMOUR AND ARMS,

CARVINGS IN IVORY,

CELTIC AND SAXON ANTIQUITIES, &c.,

OF THE

RIGHT HON. THE

EARL OF LONDESBOROUGH:

WHICH

Will be Sold by Auction, by

Messrs. CHRISTIE, MANSON & WOODS,

AT THEIR GREAT ROOMS,

8 KING STREET, ST. JAMES'S SQUARE,

On WEDNESDAY, JULY 4,

And Two following Days,

And MONDAY, JULY 9, 1888,

And Two following Days,

AT ONE O'CLOCK PRECISELY.

————◦○◦————

May be viewed Two Days preceding, and Catalogues had, at Messrs. CHRISTIE, MANSON and WOODS' Offices, 8 *King Street, St. James's Square, S.W.*

CONDITIONS OF SALE.

——o——

I. THE highest Bidder to be the Buyer; and if any dispute arise between two or more Bidders, the Lot so in dispute shall be immediately put up again and re-sold.

II. No person to advance less than 1s.; above Five Pounds, 5s.; and so on in proportion.

III. In the case of Lots upon which there is a reserve, the Auctioneer shall have the right to bid on behalf of the Seller.

IV. The Purchasers to give in their Names and Places of Abode, and to pay down 5s. in the Pound, or more, in part of payment, or the whole of the Purchase-Money, *if required*; in default of which, the Lot or Lots so purchased to be immediately put up again and re-sold.

V. The Lots to be taken away and paid for, whether genuine and authentic or not, with all faults or errors of description, at the Buyer's expense and risk, within Two days from the Sale; Messrs. CHRISTIE, MANSON and WOODS not being responsible for the correct description, genuineness, or authenticity of, or any fault or defect in, any Lot, and making no warranty whatever.

VI. To prevent inaccuracy in delivery, and inconvenience in the settlement of the Purchases, no Lot can on any account be removed during the time of Sale; and the remainder of the Purchase-Money must absolutely be paid on the delivery.

VII. Upon failure of complying with the above Conditions, the Money deposited in part of payment shall be forfeited; all Lots uncleared within the time aforesaid shall be re-sold by public or private Sale, and the deficiency (if any) attending such re-sale shall be made good by the Defaulter at this Sale.

THE LONDESBOROUGH COLLECTION.

The European Arms and Armour will be sold on Wednesday, July 4, and two following days, and may be viewed on Monday, July 2, and following day.

The Pictures will be sold on Saturday, July 7, and may be viewed three days preceding.

The Oriental Arms and Armour, Carvings in Ivory, Celtic and Saxon Antiquities, &c., will be sold on Monday, July 9, and two following days, and may be viewed on Friday, July 6, and following day.

CATALOGUE.

—•o̶ː❀ː o•—

First Day's Sale.

—•o̶ː❀ː o•—

On WEDNESDAY, JULY 4, 1888,

AT ONE O'CLOCK PRECISELY.

—•o̶ː❀ː o•—

1 FOUR SABRES; and a sword, with straight blade

2 FENCING FOIL, with chased cup; two duelling swords; and four foils

3 FOUR BAYONETS; and two swords

4 SIX SWORD BLADES

5 SABRE, used by George IV. when in the 10th Hussars, with chased silver-mounted hilt; and one, with blade engraved with the Royal Arms, with brass hilt, in scabbard, with the Prince of Wales's feathers in silver

6 INSTALLATION SWORD, of the Knights of St. Patrick

7 DRESS SWORD, with channelled and pierced blade partly engraved, the hilt of carved ivory, with shield supported by two lions, the guard terminating in lions couchant, the pommel formed of an ivory lion's head, silver wire grip

8 COUTEAU DE CHASSE, blue steel blade, partly engraved and gilt, ivory grip, and guard carved with grotesque animals with jewelled eyes

9 TWO-HANDED SWORD

10 SWORD, with blade bearing armourer's mark, the pommel formed as a grotesque head—*16th century*

11 TWO-HANDED SWORD, the blade richly engraved with coat-of-arms, crest and scrolls partly gilt, with armourer's mark, the cross guard and pommel chased with Moresque ornaments, partly gilt—*early 16th century*

From the Duc d'Abrantes' Collection

12 COURT SWORD, with Solingen blade, the hilt chased with trophies of arms partly gilt—*temp. Louis XIV.*; and one, with Colichmarde blade, and pierced and chased hilt partly gilt

13 COURT SWORD, with engraved blade with inscription, pierced silver hilt chased with heads in medallions—*temp. Louis XV.*

14 COURT SWORD, with channelled blade, the hilt inlaid with figures, birds, and scrolls of silver—*temp. Louis XIII.*

15 COURT SWORD, the hilt chased with animals and scrolls partly gilt, the sheath with steel mounts—*temp. Louis XV.*

16 COURT SWORD, with channelled and gilt blades, the hilt beautifully chased with classical figures and scrolls, and partly gilt, a chiselled fly inside the guard—*temp. Louis XV.*

17 DRESS SWORD, with gilt hilt; one, with engraved blade, the hilt inlaid with silver; and one other

18 SWORD, with chased and gilt hilt; and one, with signed blade, chased and gilt hilt—*temp. Louis XIV.*

19 DRESS SWORD, with engraved blade, the hilt inlaid with silver—*temp. Louis XIV.*; and one, the blade engraved with the arms of France, the hilt pierced and chased—*temp. Louis XVI.*

20 RAPIER, with three-edged blade engraved with ornaments, the hilt with figures and ornaments in relief

21 SMALL RAPIER, with four-edged and channelled Toledo blade, the hilt chased with masks and horses' heads partly gilt—*Italian*

22 COURT RAPIER, with four-edged blade, the hilt and pommel chiselled with combats under the walls of a fortress, in high relief

23 RAPIER, with very long blade with inscription, with shell and ring guard; and a main-gauche

24 FINE ITALIAN RAPIER, with pierced cup guard chased with figures and scrolls, chased pommel and poker blade

25 MAIN-GAUCHE, with pierced and chased grip guard, with sword breaker, pierced and chased with flowers and scrolls, the blade serrated on the back
From the Bernal Collection

26 RAPIER, with shell guard, canted pommel, very long blade; and one, with signed blade and canted pommel

27 RAPIER, with very long triangular blade, pierced shell guard and original wire grip; and one, the knuckle guard terminating in a grotesque head, the blade signed

28 SWORD, with long blade, signed and partly fluted, pierced cup guard, fluted pommel

29 SWORD, with broad fluted blade, inscribed and dated 1517, swept and pierced hilt, with shell guard, ivory grip, and pierced and engraved pommel

30 RAPIER, with signed blade, swept hilt, chased with heads in silver, and damascened with gold

31 RAPIER, blade engraved with the Spanish arms, a device and inscription, fluted swept hilt, and knurled pommel

32 RAPIER, of fine French workmanship of the end of the 16th century, with silver figures and foliage in relief on steel; at each end of the cross hilt is a mask, one end of which turns towards the pommel, the other towards the blade; in the centre are figures of Justice and Fortitude; the inside of the steel guard represents Cain slaying Abel, and Noah, with numerous animals, entering the ark; the outside, the Conversion of Saul, and the Judgment of Solomon; on the pommel is King David and Judith with the head of Holofernes; the blade is channelled and ornamented with gilt and embossed flowers, engraved edge

33 COUTEAU DE CHASSE, blade engraved with trophies of arms, with buckhorn hilt; and one, with pistol attached, hare blade, the hilt of chased brass and tortoiseshell

34 COUTEAU DE CHASSE, with signed blade, the hilt of russet steel, chased and inlaid with gold, the pommel chased with masks and festoons of fruits, in sheath, with seven hunting implements

35 COUTEAU DE CHASSE, with flint-lock pistol attached; and one, with shell guard

36 COUTEAU DE CHASSE, the pommel and cross guard chased with animals' heads; and a short sword, with broad blade

37 BOAR SWORD, with signed blade—*15th century*; and a sword, with triangular blade, spirally fluted guard and pommel—*16th century*

38 SWORD, with broad blade, partly fluted and engraved with devices, cross guard, long pear-shaped pommel, partly chased—*late 15th century*

39 KNIGHT'S SWORD, with pointed blade, engraved with trophies of arms and Tudor rose, large flat pommel and cross guard—*early 16th century*

40 RAPIER, with long blade, signed, pierced cup and chased pommel; and one, with fluted and signed blade, black shell guard and pommel

41 RAPIER, with plain cup and signed blade; and a main-gauche to match

42 PONIARD, with serrated and pierced blade of triangular form, lance-shaped point, the hilt and pommel inlaid with silver, and ornamented in relief with cherubs' heads, and elegant silver chain borders, wire handle

43 DAGGER, the hilt inlaid with masks and ornaments of silver, in velvet sheath, with mountings to match

44 PONIARD, in sheath, with a small knife and steel—*temp. Maximilian*

45 ITALIAN PONIARD, with triangular steel blade, silver corded handle, gilt pommel and hilt; the latter ornamented with filigree work; boss and guard set with imitations of precious stones; the scabbard of silver, enriched with engraved ornaments; a silver chain is attached

46 DAGGER, with fluted triangular blade, chiselled steel guard
From the Musée d'Artillerie

47 MAIN-GAUCHE, with guard pierced and chased with masks and scroll work—*temp. Louis XIII.*

48 GERMAN MACE DAGGER, plain blade, the handle bound round with copper wire, broad towards the end; engraved boss, hilt and sheath, of minute scrolls; on the extreme end of the scabbard is a large quadriform mace head with four ridges, so that when placed in its sheath the dagger answered the purpose of a mace —*early 16th century*
From the Bernal Collection

49 DAGGER, with the hilt, part of the blade and the steel mountings of the sheath richly damascened in gold with arabesques

50 DAGGER, with thumb-ring, fluted and pierced blade, the hilt engraved with a man's head and gilt, the sheath of leather, with mountings to match

51 THUMB-RING DAGGER, with triple spring blade
Used at the Tribunals of the Free Judges in Italy—16th century

52 DAGGER, with engraved blade, wheel-lock pistol attached, with gilt scroll work

53 DAGGER, with blade engraved with inscription, arms, and date 1581

54 PAIR OF PISTOLS, by Kuchenreuter, mounted with metal gilt, chased with animals and scrolls

55 SCOTCH PISTOL. with engraved lock, bearing armourer's mark, the stock with thistles and devices of engraved brass

56 THREE PISTOL BARRELS; and three spanners

57 DOUBLE WHEEL-LOCK, chased with arabesque figures, masks, and ornaments of fine Italian work

58 WHEEL-LOCK, in chiselled steel, with figures and masks in relief

59 SMALL DAG, with wheel-lock and steel butt, bearing armourer's mark

60 DAG, with three barrels and wheel-locks, the stock inlaid with figures, birds. and animals of engraved ivory and pearl

61 PISTOL, with flint-lock bayonet, war hammer and long barrel, the stock inlaid with animals and scrolls of ivory and pearl

62 HAND MORTAR, with flint-lock and brass barrel, the stock inlaid with ivory—*17th century*

63 DAG, with wheel-lock barrel, bearing armourer's mark, the stock inlaid with figures and scrolls of engraved ivory

64 WHEEL-LOCK PISTOL, with engraved lock-plate and barrel with inscription, the stock of ivory, engraved with figures and foliage, the Crucifixion on the butt

65 WHEEL-LOCK PISTOL, the lock and barrel engraved with a female figure and ornaments, the stock covered with repoussé brass work, the trigger guard chased with an arabesque figure

66 FOWLING-PIECE, with flint-lock, the barrel inlaid with scroll work of silver, the stock of ebony carved with animals, the butt inlaid with medallions of steel, with winged figures in silver—*inscription and date* 1635

67 WHEEL-LOCK GUN, the stock elaborately inlaid with St. George and the Dragon, animals and ornaments of ivory and mother-o'-pearl

68 BLUNDERBUSS, with flint-lock, the barrel partly chased and gilt, the butt covered with chased metal—*18th century*

69 WHEEL-LOCK RIFLE, lock-plate and stock inlaid with medallions of grotesque figures, of pierced and engraved brass—*17th century*

70 FLINT-LOCK RIFLE, by Simon Ruef, the stock elaborately carved with hunting subjects, Actæon, and scroll ornaments, and inlaid with a coat-of-arms carved in ivory—*dated* 1689

71 WHEEL-LOCK GUN, the barrel inlaid with maker's name, Gaspar Zelner, in gold, the lock-plate engraved with a hunting subject, the stock carved and inlaid with a coat-of-arms and ornaments of brass—*17th century*

72 WHEEL-LOCK GUN, the stock and butt inlaid with gold wire, the arms of France and cypher of Louis XIV. on the end of the butt

73 ARQUEBUS, with wheel and match-lock, the stock inlaid with St. George and the Dragon, figures, animals, and arabesques of engraved ivory, the butt engraved with a coat-of-arms, initials, and date 1611

74 Match-lock Rifle, the stock inlaid with a female figure, animals, and ornaments of engraved ivory

75 Petronel, with walnut stock, elaborately carved with figures at a repast, hunting subjects, masks, and fruits, the barrel with maker's name, Davidt Rot

76 Wheel-lock Gun, the barrel damascened with gold and silver, the stock of ebony, inlaid with ivory, engraved with heads and animals —*temp. Elizabeth*

77 Wheel-lock Gun, the barrel chased, and bearing a shield of arms, dated 1536, the stock richly inlaid with figures, animals, masks, and ornaments of engraved ivory—*German*

78 Wheel-lock Rifle, the lock-plate ornamented in bold relief and gilt, the stock inlaid with scroll ornaments of ivory, the lock chased with two lions and shields

79 Gothic Mazuelle, with steel hook to attach to saddle; and a smaller ditto

80 Battle-axe, with head engraved with a pelican, the staff engraved with arms and musical instruments, hook for saddle, the handle containing a saw and knife
From the Bernal Collection

81 Martel de Fer, engraved with figures and ornaments; and one, with saddle hook
From the Dresden Armoury

82 Martel de Fer, with bec de faucon, and octagonal shaft chased with a coat-of-arms, and with brass sides engraved with figures under Gothic canopies, and inscription—*15th century*

83 Another, of similar shape, inlaid with brass bands, and with plain shaft—*15th century*

84 Martel de Fer, with blue steel head, partly gilt, the staff covered with velvet—*Italian;* and a plain mazuelle—*temp. Edward IV.*

85 Tilting Lance, with original shaft and vamplate

86 Partisan, the blade chased with a bird in a medallion on each side, a mask, birds, and fruits—*temp. Elizabeth*
From Lord Pembroke's Collection

87 LINSTOCK, chased and engraved with original shaft; and a bridle-cutter, engraved with a knight on horseback, arms, and date 1582

88 POLE-AXE, of bright steel ; and a small pierced and engraved partisan

89 HALBERD, engraved with the arms of France

90 GUISARME—*temp. Edward IV.* ; and HALBERD, of russet gold, with pierced blade and embossed heads, original staff—*temp. Queen Elizabeth*

91 GLAIVE, blade engraved with trophies and arms of Burgundy—*dated 1660*; and a PARTISAN, the blade engraved with trophies of arms, and shield of arms with the order of the Golden Fleece

92 PAIR OF ITALIAN HALBERDS, engraved with horsemen, arabesques, and figures in medallions—*17th century*

93 THREE BITS ; and a bronze bit—*found at Dublin*

94 FIVE BITS

95 FIVE BITS

96 FOUR BITS

97 BIT, with the arms of Saxony ; and one, with pierced leaf ornament

98 PAIR OF STEEL SPURS—*temp. Charles I.*; and a pair of gilt spurs

99 LONG PRICK SPUR—*found in the Ouse;* and a pair of brass ditto

100 PAIR OF SPURS, with chains; and a pair of spurs—*temp. Charles I.*

101 PAIR OF SPURS, with large rowel ; and two others

102 PRICK SPUR ; one found at St. Albans ; and ten others

103 PAIR OF LARGE STIRRUPS, of chased steel, with animals' heads

104 PAIR OF STIRRUPS, with barred toes ; and a basket-shaped stirrup

105 PAIR OF BASKET-SHAPED STIRRUPS, inlaid with brass and silver

106 STIRRUP, of iron, inlaid with silver studs ; and a pair of perforated steel stirrups, partly gilt

107 LARGE POWDER HORN, engraved with combats of warriors, grotesque heads, and scrolls—*temp. James I.*

108 POWDER FLASK, covered with velvet, and mounted with a head in medallion, bands, and ornaments of chased metal gilt

109 SMALLER DITTO, with a figure in a medallion

110 POWDER FLASK, of wood inlaid with ivory ; and a primer, of steel and engraved bone

111 PRIMER, of metal gilt, chased with horses and classical figures ; and a round ditto, with similar subject—*Italian*

112 POWDER FLASK, of cuir bouilli, ribbed, and with masks in relief

113 CIRCULAR POWDER FLASK, of carved wood, with a boar and stag-hunt in high relief

114 POWDER FLASK, of cuir bouilli, with an animal in a medallion, and ornaments in relief

115 PATRON, of metal gilt, pierced and chased with masks, birds, and fruits—*temp. Elizabeth*

116 POWDER FLASK, of buckhorn, carved with the Last Judgment, and mounted with engraved silver

117 POWDER FLASK, of buckhorn, elaborately engraved with figures and ornaments, mantled helmet and figure of a musketeer —*temp. James I.*

118 PORTION OF A HELMET—*found at Bosworth Field*

119 LOBSTER-TAIL HELMET, with raised flutings, plume-holder, and nasal guard—*temp. Charles I.*

120 CABASSET, engraved with bands of ornaments and heads in medallions—*Italian*

121 HELMET FOR JOUSTING—*temp. Edward III.*

122 HELMET, from a church in Norfolk—*temp. King John*

123 TILTING HELMET—*temp. Henry V.*

124 HEAULME, from Wells, Norfolk—*temp. Edward I.*
      Engraved in the Journal of the British Archæological Association, Nos. 24 *and* 30

125 HIGHLAND TARGET, the brass in the centre unscrews, and shows the date 1714

126 FALLING BEAVER, in russet and gold, engraved with the device of Henry VIII., a pomegranate and lover's knot

127 CHAPEAU DE FER—*temp. Henry VIII.*
      From the Bernal Collection

128 SADDLE BACK, of steel, chased with fleurs-de-lys and scrolls, partly gilt

129 LANTERN SHIELD, of cuir bouilli, with a seated figure of a warrior and Victory in relief—*Italian*

131 CHAMFRON, of steel, with testière, ornamented with chased and gilt trophies of arms

132 TILTING PAULDRON, with pass guard, in russet steel and gold, etched on the lower part with a combat, scrolls, and trophies— *German*

133 GORGET, with chased and gilt dragons and scrolls, corded border, the arms of Antwerp in the centre

134 CUIRASS, consisting of breast plate and back plate inlaid with gold—*temp. Charles I.*

135 LOBSTER-TAILED HELMET, engraved with ornaments—*temp. Charles I.*

136 SHIELD, of triangular form, with St. George and the Dragon in repoussé work

137 CIRCULAR SHIELD, of steel, engraved with foliage and busts

138 A PLAIN VISORED HELMET, of rare form—*temp. Maximilian*

139 FRONT OF A GORGET, of repoussé work, with a figure of a knight of St. George on horseback, cherubs and arabesques richly engraved and coated with silver—*Italian, temp. Elizabeth*

140 BACK-PLATE, made for a siege, with narrow bands inlaid with gold —*Italian or Spanish, temp. James II.*

141 SHIELD, repoussé in lozenges, engraved with Moresque ornaments and partly gilt—*Spanish*

142 SHIELD OF BRONZE, with embossed ornaments—*Celtic*
Found at Athenry, County Donegal

143 BUCKLER OR TARGET, of wood, of square form, covered with parchment, and with hook to attach it to the girdle—*temp. Maximilian*

144 TOP-PLATE OF A TASSET, chased with masks and ornaments, and damascened with gold

145 SUIT OF ARMOUR, cap-à-pie, beautifully channelled and engraved with semicircles, lions' or leopards' heads and lions rampant, all which have been originally gilt. This suit, comprising all the pieces necessary for war or for a tournament, is very remarkable for its completeness.

The mounted suit consists of a helmet, with a ridge, visor and beaver, gorget, with lapping plates, breast and back plates, with lance rest; the gusset under the right arm protected by a roundel, right and left pauldrons, rere braces, vambraces and gauntlets, cuisses and jambs. A jupon of chain mail is seen from beneath the tassets; the boots also of chain mail, with steel toes. The extra pieces are—

1. The grande garde for tournaments, consisting of the mentonnière and placcate, covered by a large manteau d'armes, chased with lions' heads

2. A light kind of helmet, with visor

3. A volant piece, or extra protection for the neck and face

4. A helmet, with an umbril over the forehead, a high crest or comb, and an ear-piece, pierced with holes

5. A pièce de renfort for back of helmet

6. An extra pauldron, with a raised pass-guard to protect the neck from the edge of the lance

7. Garde-bras for the left elbow

8. A reinforcing breastplate, with tassets and flange for the tournament

9. A circular shield, embossed with rampant lions

10. A straight sword

11. A chamfron for a horse's head

12. The cantle of a saddle

Probably of Italian work, about 1550
From the Bernal Collection

146 SUIT OF ARMOUR, with bands engraved with winged and other figures, animals, masks, and ornaments: consisting of helmet, gorget, espaulières, rere braces, elbow guards, long gauntlets, backplate, breastplate, engraved with a knight in devotion and the Crucifixion, long tassets, jambs, and sollerets—*circa* 1530–50

147 SUIT OF TILTING ARMOUR, with bands engraved with a running pattern of branches with fruit and foliage; helmet with a volant piece for attaching to breastplate, gorget, espaulières, rere braces, vambraces, elbow guards, backplate, breastplate with flange, tilting bridle, gauntlet with elbow guard, short tassets, skirt of chain mail, cuisses and jambs—*temp. Phillip and Mary*

From the Amoria Reale at Madrid

End of First Day's Sale.

Second Day's Sale.

On THURSDAY, JULY 5, 1888,

AT ONE O'CLOCK PRECISELY.

155 Two CLAYMORES, one with fluted Andrea Ferrara blade, and one with plain blade, engraved with inscription

156 Two CLAYMORES, one with Andrea Ferrara blade

157 CLAYMORE, with Andrea Ferrara blade, marked with four negro heads—*17th century*

158 CLAYMORE, with fluted blade, engraved with inscription—*temp. George III.*

159 Two CLAYMORES, one with fluted Andrea Ferrara blade, and one with a medallion of a crowned thistle in the hilt

160 MORTUARY SWORD, the blade inscribed " for my king and country "; and one, with pierced shell guard—*17th century*

161 Two SWORDS, with cross hilts

162 Two DITTO

163 SWORD, with broad blade bearing Julian del Rey's mark, the hilt engraved and partly gilt

164 HUNTING SWORD, with saw-back blade, signed Clemens Willems, Solingen, and pierced shell guard, engraved

165 SWORD, with long blade, channelled and signed, the hilt and guard with chiselled steel negro heads

166 SWORD, with serrated blade, inscribed Morgenland, Hispania, armourer's mark of the three kings' heads

C

167 SWORD, with cross guard formed as fleurs-de-lys; and rapier, with blade, signed Sahagum, and cup hilt

168 TWO-HANDED SWORD, with flame blade—*Swiss, temp. Elizabeth*

169 TWO-HANDED SWORD, with flame blade, bearing armourer's mark, the guard terminating in fleurs-de-lys

170 TWO-HANDED SWORD, the blade signed Zinser

171 TWO-HANDED SWORD-BLADE, with armourer's mark

172 COUTEL, or Short Sword, slightly curved, with semicircular guard attached to the cross hilt, which turns over at each end towards the blade, twisted wire grip. The guard hilt and pommel are of steel inlaid with gold scrolls, and on each side of the centre of the hilt is a medallion representing a wild-boar hunt. The blade is also damascened with gold on the lower part, with a view of the siege of Boulogne, which took place in 1513, exhibiting the cannon, ammunition, waggons, and temporary fortifications and soldiers, the reverse side bears the following inscription :

HENRICI OCTAVI LETARE, BOLONIA, DVCTV,
PVRPVREIS TVRRES CONSPICIENDA ROSIS,
JAM TRACTA JACENT MALE OLENTIA LILIA, PVLSVS
GALLVS, ET INVICTA REGNAT IN ARCE LEO :
SIC TIBI NEC VIRTVS DEERIT, NEC GRATIA FORMÆ,
CVM LEO TVTELA, CVM ROSA SIT DECORI.

This interesting sword is traditionally reported to have belonged to Henry VIII. Length, 2 ft. 2 in.

Engraved in Fairholt's ' Miscellanea Graphica,' pl. xxvii. fig. 1

173 SWORD, with triangular blade, cross guard, and hilt—*early 16th century*

174 SWORD, the blade engraved with figures in medallions, grotesque animals, and scrolls, the hilt of brass, chased with foliage and trophies of arms, and motto " Che Sara "—*temp. Phillip and Mary*

175 SWORD, with blade engraved with ornaments, and dated 1630, the grip of chased steel, inlaid with silver, and with modern brass guard

176 KNIGHT's SWORD, with cross guard and plain pommel—*early 16th century*

177 SHORT SWORD, with broad triangular blade and wheel pommel

178 SHORT KNIGHT's SWORD (Estoc), with wheel pommel—*early 14th century—found in the Thames*

179 TWO TWO-HANDED SWORDS, for tournaments; one, with engraved blade

180 EXECUTIONER's SWORD, with channelled blade, chased hilt and leather sheath, with steel end inscribed I.H.S.

181 EXECUTIONER's SWORD, with broad scimitar-shaped blade, the guard in the form of a serpent, the steel grip indented for fingers, elaborately engraved with the guilloche pattern and scrolls partly gilt. The blade inscribed in engraved and gilt letters (Lombardic), " I.H.S. AUTEM TRANSIENS PER MEDEON INLORON INBAT." The armourer's mark on the blade is three fleurs-de-lys—*15th century*
From the Bernal Collection

182 EXECUTIONER's SWORD, with very broad blade engraved with flowers, boxwood handle carved with animals, and an inscription in Gothic letters, in a scabbard with steel mounts

183 RAPIER, with signed blade, minutely pierced cup, and pear-shaped pommel, opening with a spring, to contain despatches
From the Bernal Collection

184 RAPIER, with broad blade, inscribed Pace Porto, Guera Cercho, cup guard pierced and chased with flowers and scrolls, the pommel chased with figures and foliage

185 RAPIER, the cup guard chased and pierced with the Adoration of the Shepherds and the Flight into Egypt, the pommel beautifully chiselled with knights in armour, on horseback—*17th century*

186 RAPIER, pierced Spanish blade, signed, the hilt chiselled in high relief with figures, the pommel chased with battle scenes in compartments

c 2

187 RAPIER, with engraved blade bearing arms, the swept guard and straight quillons formed in imitation of a square-linked chain studded with silver beads, the grip engraved, square pommel chased with a figure on each side, and lions' heads at the angles

188 RAPIER, with signed blade, and swept hilt chased with scallop shells, and with chased pommel; and one, with pierced shell guard, and spirally twisted pommel, the hilt partly gilt

189 DAGGER, with agate handle, chased steel blade, and silver-mounted sheath; a stiletto; and a dagger, with steel-mounted sheath

190 PONIARD, with channelled and pierced blade, carved ivory hilt, with two monsters and figure of a knight in armour—*17th century*

191 STILETTO, with ivory handle, formed as a seated female figure, silver-mounted sheath

192 DAGGER, with curious square blade inlaid with gold, knotted wood hilt, and sheath mounted with ivory—*Italian*

193 DAGGER, the blade engraved with emblems and inscription, "Les chastes liens d'amour," ivory handle inlaid with figures of silver wire

194 DAGGER, with chased and gilt steel hilt—*temp. Louis XV.,* the sheath silver mounted; and a dagger, with mother-o'-pearl grip mounted with chased metal gilt—*of the time of the Empire*

195 DAGGER, the blade engraved with ornaments and Italian inscription, the cross guard inlaid with figures and fruits in silver, the grip of cut steel, in sheath

196 DAGGER, the blade partly engraved and gilt, the hilt of steel, engraved with ornaments, the mountings of sheath to match—*Italian*

197 STILETTO, with blue steel blade inlaid with gold, pierced ivory hilt, formed as four snakes entwined, inlaid with gold and minutely engraved

198 DAGGER, with four-edged blade, the grip inlaid with gold, and with ebony pommel; and one, with saw-back blade, pierced and chased grip and pommel, brass guard

199 DAGGER, with ivory hilt, carved with figures of Adam and Eve, blade with armourer's mark

200 DAGGER, with engraved and gilt blade, with armourer's mark, ivory hilt formed as a group of Venus and Cupid

201 ANELACE, with engraved blade and brass handle, inlaid with ebony and ivory

202 ANELACE, or Dagger, with an ivory handle and short hilt bent towards the blade, with plain silver tips ; on the handle are inserted perforated silver circles of geometrical tracery. The blade is straight, double-edged and slightly fluted, 1 ft. 5 in. long, 3 in. wide next the handle, tapering to a point. It is engraved on one side with a man in a jerkin, tight hose, and drawn sword, and inscribed "INJURIA LACESSITUS" (*sic*) ; on the other, a man sheathing a sword, and "IRAM COMPRIME."

203 PAIR OF DUELLING PISTOLS, by Devismes, Paris, with ebony stock, and mounted with engraved silver gilt ; a pair of very small pistols, by the same maker ; two bullet moulds ; and other implements

204 PAIR OF PISTOLS, of the Imperial manufactory, the trigger guards and end of butts of silver, chased with trophies of arms
Presented by Napoleon I. to Marshal Marmont

205 PISTOL, with flint-lock barrel and steel butt inlaid with scrolls and flowers in gold

206 PAIR OF PISTOLS, by Domenico Bonomino, mounted in chiselled steel, with the labours of Hercules in high relief, the triggers formed as monkeys, and at the end of the ramrods Atlas bearing a globe

207 PAIR OF PISTOLS, by Lazzarino Comminazzo, with flint locks richly chiselled and engraved, the stocks mounted with masks and scroll work of steel

208 PAIR OF PISTOLS, with flint-locks, engraved barrels, the stocks inlaid with grotesque figures, animals, and scrolls of ivory and mother-o'-pearl

209 DAG, with double wheel-lock, bearing armourer's mark, and steel butt—*temp. Elizabeth*

210 PISTOL, with flint-lock and barrel inlaid with gold, the stock inlaid with foliage and scrolls of silver, and with a coat-of-arms

211 PAIR OF WHEEL-LOCK PISTOLS, the barrels engraved with scrolls, the stocks inlaid with ivory, the butts with a trophy of arms in repoussé brasswork

212 PAIR OF FLINT-LOCK PISTOLS, the barrels inlaid with birds in gold, the stocks of ivory carved as Turks' heads

213 SNAP-HAUNCE PISTOL, the stock inlaid with brass

214 PISTOL, with wheel-lock, the barrel and stock of steel chased with scroll ornaments

215 ANOTHER, nearly similar

216 WHEEL-LOCK PISTOL, with long barrel, the stock inlaid with figures and animals of ivory—*temp. Elizabeth*

217 FIVE FLINT-LOCK MUSKETS

218 WHEEL-LOCK RIFLE, the barrel partly gilt, the stock inlaid with St. George and the Dragon, animals, and ornaments of engraved ivory—*16th century*

219 WHEEL-LOCK GUN, with short barrel bearing armourer's mark, the stock inlaid with ivory

220 WHEEL-LOCK RIFLE, the barrel and lock engraved and bearing the armourer's mark, the stock inlaid with equestrian figures engaged in combat, and animals of green ivory and mother-o'-pearl—*German, 17th century*

221 MATCH-LOCK GUN, the stock inlaid with mother-o'-pearl

222 FLINT-LOCK GUN, the butt covered with repoussé steel work, and with long barrel bearing armourer's mark—*Italian, 17th century*

223 ANOTHER, of similar design

224 ARQUEBUS, with sight chased with a Turk's head, long barrel with match-lock, the stock inlaid with hunting subjects and a view of a city in medallions of engraved ivory, and with flowers and ornaments of mother-o'-pearl and ivory—*German, 17th century*

225 WHEEL-LOCK RIFLE, the barrel with armourer's mark, and dated 1762, the butt inlaid with silver scrolls, medallions of hunting scenes and coat-of-arms

226 MATCH-LOCK GUN, the barrel chiselled in high relief with a man blowing a horn, hounds and stag, the stock inlaid with knights in armour, Judith with the head of Holofernes; and a lady in costume of the 16th century, buildings and dogs of ivory

227 WHEEL-LOCK RIFLE, the stock inlaid with hunting subjects in ivory and mother-o'-pearl

228 BATTLE-AXE, with bec de faucon; and a plain battle-axe—*15th century*

229 BATTLE-AXE, blue steel, inlaid with gold, with armorial bearings and motto—*15th century*

230 BATTLE-AXE, the head chased with knights on horseback; and a martel de fer

231 GERMAN MINER'S STAFF, partly of ivory, engraved with figures, and with gilt head

232 MARTEL DE FER, with pierced hammer and original staff

233 BATTLE-HAMMER, with three spikes; and a morning star

234 RANSEUR—*found in the Cambridge Fens*

235 GLAIVE OF STATE, with very large engraved blade, it was carried at the head of the Doge's gallery
From Lord Pembroke's Collection

236 VENETIAN BILL, slightly engraved, with original staff; and a plain halberd—*temp. Elizabeth*

237 ENGRAVED SPEAR, with triple blade forming a partisan, in hollow shaft, with spring formed as a bust
From the Bernal Collection

238 HALBERD, pierced and engraved with masks, partly gilt—*temp. Elizabeth*

239 GLAIVE, richly engraved and gilt, with original shaft

240 PARTISAN, engraved with ornaments, and with original shaft

241 GLAIVE, blade engraved with arms, and original staff studded with brass—*early 16th century*

242 Two HALBERDS

243 BILL, with flame spike; and one, with plain blade

244 BILL, the blade with armourer's mark and inscription; and one, with plain blade—*temp. Henry VIII.*

245 GERMAN HUNTING FORK; an Irish pike; and an axe

246 PAIR OF SPURS, engraved and silvered; and a pair, with figures in silver in relief

247 PAIR OF SPURS, inlaid with figures and ornaments of silver; and a pair of gilt spurs

248 SPUR, of polished steel; and a pair of engraved steel spurs

249 PAIR OF GILT SPURS; and a pair, inlaid with masks and ornaments of silver

From the Bernal Collection

250 PAIR OF CHASED STEEL SPURS—*temp. Charles I.;* and a pair of engraved spurs

251 GUARDED STEEL STIRRUP—*found in the Thames;* and a pair of bronze spurs

252 TWO PAIRS OF MEXICAN SPURS

253 PAIR OF MOORISH PRICK-SPURS; and a pair of Spanish spurs

254 PAIR OF SPURS, of chased and pierced steel; and a spur—*found at Wexford*

255 PAIR OF MEXICAN SPURS; and a pair, smaller

256 MOORISH SPIKE SPUR; a brass spur; and five others

257 PAIR OF MOORISH SHOE STIRRUPS, of bronze; and a pair, of stamped leather

258 PAIR OF MUSSULMAN'S SPANISH STIRRUPS, pierced and chased with figures, animals, and scroll work—*of very early date*

259 CROSSBOW, the stock inlaid with ivory, engraved with the figure of a bishop, masks and ornaments, coat-of-arms and date

260 CROSSBOW, the stock carved with figures and animals, and inlaid with engraved ivory

261 SMALL CROSSBOW, the stock inlaid with engraved ivory—*dated* 1646

262 PROD, of dark wood, with sphynx handle, steel bow, and a spike issuing from a lion's mouth at the end

263 MOULINET, engraved with ornaments, and dated 1612

264 ARBALEST, the steel bow painted with hunting subjects and coats-of-arms in colours, on gold ground, the stock square, the sides inlaid with scrolls and flowers in coloured marqueterie, the back and front inlaid with figures, masks, portraits, and arms of engraved ivory, the butt bearing a cartouche, with initials and date 1572

From the Bernal Collection

265 HEAULME—*temp. Richard II.*

266 TILTING HELMET OF SIR JOHN CROSBY
From St. Helen's Church, London
Engraved in Stothard's ' Monumental Effigies '

267 HELMET, engraved with ornaments—*temp. Phillip and Mary—found at Flodden Field*
Formerly in the possession of Sir W. Scott, and represented in his portrait

268 HEAULME—*temp. Henry III.*
From Mayfield Church, Sussex

269 HEAULME OF SIR JOHN DE BOTTELER—*from a church in Bedfordshire where his tomb exists—temp. Henry VI.*

270 HEAULME, said to be that of Sir Aylmer de Valence whose widow founded Pembroke College—*found at Denmey Abbey, near Cambridge*

271 HEAULME, from a castle in Bavaria

272 BASCINET, with camail attached—*temp. Richard II.*

273 HAUBERK, of chain mail, with a cross formed of brass rings—*from a tomb in Norfolk*

274 EARLY FLEMISH TILTING-SHIELD, painted with arms and a female figure

275 NECK SHIELD, painted with a coat-of-arms

276 FLUTED BRASSART—*temp. Maximilian*

277 BACK-PIECE, with garde reins attached—*temp. Henry VII.*

278 BRIDLE GAUNTLET, of steel—*temp. Henry VII.*

279 VAMPLATE, or guard of steel, for a tilting spear—*temp. Henry VI.*

280 CHAPEAU DE FER—*temp. Henry IV.*

281 CANTLE OF A SADDLE, of damascened repoussé work, a female standing on a dolphin, above are two heads of Æolus
From Lord Pembroke's Collection

282 MORION, with high comb, engraved with fleurs-de-lys

283 PORTION OF A SMALL SUIT OF ARMOUR : consisting of breast-plate and tassets of overlapping plates of steel, with engraved borders, the breast-plate engraved with the Annunciation and two saints, an inscription beneath

284 STEEL BACK-PLATE

285 Two OBLONG PLAQUES, of repoussé work, richly gilt, with combats of warriors—*Italian*

286 FLUTED HELMET, with long lobster tail, curious guard for the face, ear-pieces of Eastern character

287 HELMET, with visor, richly engraved and gilt with monogram —*temp. Queen Elizabeth*

288 PAIR OF MECHANICAL HANDS, in wrought iron—*very rare*

289 HELMET, with fluted crown and perforated visor—*temp. Charles I.*

290 BACK OF A GORGET, chased with a skirmish of cavalry in a medallion, inlaid with silver, and engraved with military trophies —*temp. Charles I.*
From Alton Towers

291 HELMET, engraved with bands of ornaments, with visor—*temp. Elizabeth*

292 BACK-PLATE, engraved with arabesques, vine leaves, and figures —*German, temp. Maximilian*

293 CIRCULAR SHIELD, studded with bronze bosses, with iron centre

294 LANCE REST, of steel

295 GOTHIC CHAMFRON

296 PAIR OF STEEL GAUNTLETS, richly damascened with military weapons, arquebuses, palm branches and garlands, divided by silver cords and knots—*Spanish work, 16th century*

297 PAIR OF PAGE'S STEEL GAUNTLETS, chased and damascened with gold arabesques and scrolls; on the wrist of each a figure of Mars—*16th century*

298 TASSET AND PORTION OF AN ESPAULIÈRE, of hammered steel, with alternate ropes and puffs in engraved and gilt borders

299 SHIELD, of circular form, of cuir bouilli of the 16th century, with figures and ornaments in relief. In the centre Perseus and Andromeda, and four smaller medallions of Mercury, Venus, &c., foliated scrolls, between which are winged genii and military trophies. The interior of the shield decorated with emblematical medallions and a coat-of-arms, *gules*, a lion rampant, *or*, holding a fleur-de-lys of the same, in a glass frame, and on mahogany pillar

From Strawberry Hill

300 MENTONNIÈRE, with manteau d'armes attached, engraved with scrolls and borders richly gilt, with enamelled shield of Saxony, and with helmets and crests in elaborate mantling, underneath are the letters F.S.V.

301 STEEL MORION, repoussé, on one side a camp scene, on the other a combat; it is likewise ornamented with a mask and reclining figures, arabesque scrolls on the crest or comb, which is much higher than usual. It has been originally damascened with gold, portions of which still remain in the interstices— *Milanese, 16th century work*

302 PAGE'S SUIT, russet, with gilt bands: consisting of breastplate, backplate, gorget, rere and vambraces, gauntlets and long tassets to detach

303 FOLDING STEEL CHAIR, resting on cross-pieces, so constructed as to take asunder readily for use, probably during a campaign, it is secured by screws and hooks, the seat being made of leather stretched over two metal rollers. The open floriated metal ornament is boldly designed, the scrolls on the solid parts of the chair relieved by gilding—*Spanish, 17th century—3 ft. 2 in. high, 2 ft. 3 in. wide*

Engraved in Fairholt's ' Miscellanea Graphica '

304 BREASTPLATE, of steel repoussé work, richly damascened with gold, gilt background, and inlaid with silver. In the centre at top is a gorgon's head, beneath which are two captives seated on an arch, supported by therms, and a statue of Mars, resting on the heads of two fauns ; on either side are festoons and masks, medallions of Jupiter, Mercury, Saturn, and Apollo, trophies, satyrs, &c. Date circa 1550. This breastplate is said to have been worn by Philip IV. of Spain

From the Bernal Collection

Engraved in Fairholt's ' Miscellanea Graphica,' pl. xxxix. fig. 2

305 PAIR OF STEEL GAUNTLETS, in repoussé, damascened with gold, in the centre of each is a figure of Mars, with captives and trophies at the sides, part of the same suit as the preceding

From the Bernal Collection

End of Second Day's Sale.

Third Day's Sale.

On FRIDAY, JULY 6, 1888,

AT ONE O'CLOCK PRECISELY.

311 MATADORE's SWORD, the blade with armourer's mark, inscription and date 1769; and a plain sword, formerly used by the Matadore Montes, made at Toledo 1835

312 SWORD, with broad blade engraved with a Maltese cross; and a hunting sword, with engraved blade and hilt

313 SWORD, with broad channelled hilt chased and terminating in negro heads

314 SWORD AND DAGGER, made for Francesco Padilla, one of Charles V.'s generals

315 SWORD, with short broad blade, cross hilt, chased with figures, pommel formed as a negro's head

316 EXECUTIONER's SWORD, with short blade engraved with figures and flowers; and a cutlass, the hilt formed as a bear and ragged staff

317 SCHIAVONA, with basket hilt, used by the Doge's guard; and a rapier, with plain cup and signed blade

318 FIGHTING SWORD, blade bearing armourer's mark, straight guard and openwork pommel, originally gilt

319 EXECUTIONER's SWORD, with broad blade with German inscription and date 1688, fluted hilt and pommel silvered

320 ANOTHER, the blade bearing armourer's mark, chased brass hilt and pommel

321 SMALLER DITTO, the blade engraved with the Crucifixion, emblems, and inscription

322 RAPIER, with channelled and signed blade, gilt hilt of unusual form, chased with two masks and birds, and large spirally fluted pommel

From the Duke of Sussex's Collection

323 SWORD, with chiselled steel hilt; and rapier, with pierced hilt chased with scrolls

324 SWORD, with short blade engraved with a lion rampant, masks and trophies, dated 1600, the hilt pierced; and a sword, with engraved blade, dated 1657, the hilt inlaid with silver

325 SWORD, the blade inscribed Solo Deo Gloria, the hilt ornamented with laureated heads; and a sword, with signed blade engraved with a fox

326 SWORD, with fluted Andrea Ferrara blade, basket hilt inlaid with silver, Lord Fairfax's sword

From Sir Cuthbert Sharpe's Collection

327 SWORD, with Solingen blade, swept hilt with wheel-lock pistol attached: and a sword, with swept hilt

328 SWORD, with broad channelled blade, blue steel hilt; and a rapier, with long blade and fluted pommel

329 SWORD WITH CROSS HILT, double-edged, the hilt ornamented with medallions of Leda and the Swan, and other classical subjects in damascened gold, with silver-studded frames; the handle bound round with a fine chain. The blade inscribed on one side NO·ME·SAGVES·SIN·RASON, and on the other NO·ME·ENDAINES· SIN·HONOR, and the name Manel Gosalel, probably that of the armourer—*17th century, Spanish*

330 RAPIER, with long blade, fluted and signed, pierced shell guard, hilt with scrolls and letter S.—*temp. Charles I.*

331 SWORD, with folding blade, engraved with a French inscription and ornaments

332 RAPIER, with pierced shell guard and fluted pommel, the blade signed; and one, with three-ring guard and signed blade

333 RAPIER, with shell and three-ring guard, fluted pommel and signed blade; and one, with fluted pommel and signed blade

334 RAPIER, with pierced shell and three-ring guard, Solingen blade; and a rapier, with signed blade

335 RAPIER, with pierced shell guard, signed blade; and a rapier, with pierced cup hilt and fluted pommel

336 RAPIER, with fluted and inscribed blade, swept hilt and pommel chased and engraved with masks and scrolls

337 RAPIER, with fluted and pierced blade, signed Antonio Piclionio in Toledo, pierced and engraved cup and pommel

338 RAPIER, with pierced and engraved cup, pierced grip and chased pommel

339 RAPIER, blade partly fluted and signed, ringed guard and pommel, chased with scale-pattern ornaments, and inlaid with silver

340 VERY FINE RAPIER, the hilt, pommel, and basket ornamented with inlaid silver trophies, animals, busts, and flowers, the grip silver gilt, engraved with trophies; the blade two-edged and fluted, inscribed on one side, HEINRICH DINGER ME FECIT; on the other, HEINRICH DINGER SOLIGEN; the armourer's mark an anchor with a double cross above

341 PONIARD, with broad blade, in metal-gilt sheath pierced and chased with figures of warriors, terminating in a grotesque mask — *temp. Maximilian*

342 PONIARD, with broad blade, in gilt sheath chased with Jepthah and numerous other figures in high relief—*Italian, 16th century*

343 DAGGER, with four-edged blade and double cross hilt

344 DAGGER, with twisted cross hilt; and one, of similar form, with chased hilt

345 MISERICORDE, with a triangular fluted blade, gilt. On the sides are engraved female figures, with the high-horned head dress and costume of the latter part of the fourteenth century. On the back is an abbreviated inscription; the words divided by flowers; a chequered pattern at the point; the grip is of wood; the pommel and cross hilt formed of chevron bands, hatched and gilt

Fairholt's 'Miscellanea Graphica,' pl. xiii fig. 6

346 Stiletto, the hilt formed as the figure of a warrior, partly silvered ; and a plain stiletto

347 Dagger, with silver ball hilt and cross guard

348 Dagger, the blade engraved with figures and ornaments, with agate hilt, silver mounted

349 Plug Bayonet, the blade with armourer's mark, partly gilt and engraved, the hilt of ivory, inlaid with silver

350 Dagger, forming a pair of compasses, with scales on the blade, and inscription, the hilt inlaid with gold

351 Poniard, the hilt ornamented with niello work, and terminating in two winged ornaments, chased with a figure, and with military trophies ; and one, of similar form, partly chased and gilt, in sheath

352 Poniard, the guard and pommel chased with combats of equestrian figures—*temp. Elizabeth*, modern blade, by Crevelli of Milan

353 Main-gauche, with serrated blade and knuckle guard, engraved with flowers ; and one, with sword-breaker, blade with armourer's mark and shell guard

354 Main-gauche, with curious serrated and combed blade, the hilt with perforated guard and pommel, the quillons terminating in strawberries

355 Dagger, with thumb-ring, the blade engraved with an inscription and arms, and with armourer's mark ; and one, with swept guard

356 Pair of Scotch Pistols, with flint-locks and steel butts, with brass crest—*18th century*

357 Pistol, with flint-lock and brass stock ; and one, with steel stock

358 Pistol, with flint-lock for two charges, the stock inlaid with silver, brass crest at the end of butt ; and a pair of double-barrel flint-lock pistols, inlaid with gold

359 Pair of Pistols, by Kuchenreuter ; and four others

360 Pistol, with wheel-lock and hatchet attached, bearing armourer's mark, long stock inlaid with ivory

361 Pistol, with wheel-lock, the stock inlaid with figures and animals of engraved ivory and pearl, the end of the butt engraved with a coat-of-arms

362 PISTOL, with wheel-lock and barrel, dated 1570, the stock elaborately inlaid with figures, animals, and scrolls of ivory

363 PISTOL, with wheel-lock, barrel bearing armourer's mark, the stock inlaid with birds and scroll work of ivory, a warrior's head carved at the end of the butt

364 WHEEL-LOCK PISTOL, with barrel bearing armourer's mark and initials, the stock minutely inlaid with ivory scroll work

365 WHEEL-LOCK PISTOL, barrel with armourer's marks, the stock inlaid with scroll ornaments of ivory

366 WHEEL-LOCK PISTOL, the lock partly engraved and gilt, the stock covered with leather and inlaid with grotesque figures of ivory a chasing of St. George and the Dragon on end of the stock
From the Royal Armoury, Dresden

367 Two PISTOLS, similar

368 PETRONEL, with rifled barrel, by Andreas Brantner, the lock and plate chased with scrolls and flowers

369 RIFLE BARREL, chiselled in high relief, with figures in costume — *temp. Phillip and Mary*

370 RIFLE BARREL, with sight, chased with three figures in medallions and ornaments

371 MATCH-LOCK RIFLE, the stock inlaid with mother-o'-pearl

372 BLUNDERBUSS, with flint-lock, the barrel bearing armourer's mark, the stock of ebony inlaid with silver scroll work

373 CARBINE, or Gun with a wide bore, the stock and butt carved with scroll work, and ornamented with gilt-metal mountings, on which occur a medallion containing a portrait bust and emblematical figures; on the side of the butt is an engraved silver plate, with a portrait of Charles Albert, Duke of Bavaria, on horseback; the lower part of the barrel is inlaid with a silver figure of the Virgin and Child, a laurel branch, and the interlaced cipher "C.H.," surmounted by a ducal coronet, on either side a trophy of arms; the barrel is rifled with spiral channels —*temp. William and Mary*

374 HEAVY ARQUEBUS, the stock inlaid with a grotesque figure and animals, in engraved ivory, initials H.R.S. 1651

D

375 WHEEL-LOCK GUN, the stock formed as a crosier, inlaid with the arms of Burgundy, monogram A.H.S. and crown in engraved ivory

376 LARGE WHEEL-LOCK GUN, the stock elaborately inlaid with hunting subjects, horsemen, and figures, with musical instruments of engraved ivory—*dated* 1609

377 ARQUEBUS, with wheel-lock, the stock laid over with repoussé brass work, trophies, figures, and cherubs' heads, monogram and crown

378 WHEEL-LOCK RIFLE, to be loaded at the breech, the stock carved with a dolphin's head and masks, the lock chiselled with grotesque animals, the butt inlaid with ivory, pearl, and ebony —*Italian*

379 PETRONEL, the stock inlaid with lions' heads, medallions and flowers of engraved ivory—*German*

380 SIEGE MATCH-LOCK GUN, the stock inlaid with mother-o'-pearl, engraved with classical subjects and hunting scenes

381 WHEEL-LOCK GUN, the stock and butt inlaid with ivory, tinted green and brown, engraved with reclining figures of Venus. Diana, and other deities, flowers and arabesques; on the back are representations of " David," " Maccabæus," and " Carolus ; " the barrel is inlaid with gold and silver scrolls—*length, 4 ft. 3 in.* —16*th century*

   From the Debruge Collection

382 WHEEL-LOCK GUN, the stock inlaid with ivory and pearl—*German* *From Lord Pembroke's Collection*

383 WHEEL-LOCK GUN, the butt inlaid with ivory, engraved with a man on horseback, bear and dogs, men, birds, Cupid on a hippogriff; the butt is shaped to fit the fingers; the lock damascened with gold and silver ; the lower part of the barrel ornamented with strap-work, masks, and flowers in high relief, the upper part damascened with heads of the Cæsars, Mars with trophies, and Hercules and Cerberus. On the end of the butt is inserted a silver medal, inscribed " Sanctus Rudbertus Epis Salisb · 1623 "—*length, 4 ft. 4½ in.*

384 Two MORNING STARS, one with wood staff

385 MACE, the head formed with fleurs-de-lys and engraved staff; and a battle hammer, the staff inlaid with ivory

386 MAZUELLE, inlaid with silver scrolls and gold bands—*Italian*

387 MACE, with pierced and ornamented head, spirally twisted steel shaft

388 BATTLE-AXE, with original staff, the head inlaid with circles of brass—*15th century*

389 BATTLE-AXE; and a shaped blade

390 VOUGE, the blade pierced and inlaid with the Tudor rose in metal —*15th century*

391 VOUGE, with pierced blade—*15th century*

392 LOCHABER AXE, with original studded staff, the blade with armourer's mark; and a battle-axe—*15th century*

393 MARTEL DE FER, said to have belonged to Edward IV.
From the Musée d'Artillerie, Paris

394 Two HALBERDS, chased with figures and ornaments

395 HALBERD, with openwork steel head—*temp. Queen Elizabeth;* and HALBERD, with a gilt sun with rays on each side—*temp. Charles I.*

396 STATE HALBERD, blue steel gilt, with arms of France and cypher of Louis XIV.

397 MUZZLE, with coat-of-arms and initials

398 MUZZLE, of steel and brass, engraved—*dated* 1589

399 MUZZLE, of steel, with engraved foliage pattern

400 MASK, representing a grotesque human head, with ass' ears

401 MASK, of perforated and engraved steel work, with inscriptions, and dated 1549, and with grotesque heads in relief, bearing rings

402 FELON'S BRAND; and an iron collar, with small spikes and brass bosses
From Mozambique

403 MASK OF PUNISHMENT

404 MASK, of hammered steel, probably used by an executioner

405 CATCH-POLE

From the Castle at Nuremberg

406 STEEL INSTRUMENT, for opening the mouth

407 BODICE, of openwork steel—*17th century*

408 GAG OF IRON ; thumbscrew, of engraved steel ; a plain ditto ; and collar of torture, with spikes inside and out

409 PAIR OF STIRRUPS, of metal gilt, chased with arabesque figures, masks, and ornaments

410 PAIR OF STIRRUPS, of metal gilt, chased with figures ; and a mask —*16th century*

411 PAIR OF STEEL STIRRUPS, pierced and twisted—*16th century*

412 STIRRUP, with toecap ; one, of perforated steel ; and one, inlaid with silver and brass

413 PAIR OF STIRRUPS, of metal gilt, chased with scrolls; perforated steel stirrup ; and a stirrup—*found at Fenny-Stratford*

414 STIRRUP, of perforated steel, chased with trophies of arms and masks ; and an engraved steel stirrup, partly gilt

415 POWDER FLASK, of metal gilt, chased with a hunting subject, the back engraved with scrolls

416 POWDER FLASK, of buckhorn, carved with two figures ; and one, silver mounted, carved with a cross and scrolls

417 CIRCULAR POWDER FLASK, of wood, with pierced centre inlaid with ivory, mounted with engraved metal

418 TWO SMALLER DITTO

419 PATRON, of wood, minutely inlaid with ivory, and with steel mounts ; and a small primer, of chased brass

420 PRIMER, of metal gilt, chased with a combat of horsemen ; and a steel flask, inlaid with figures and ornaments in silver

421 POWDER HORN, carved with figures, animals, and landscape ; and portion of a flask, of buckhorn, carved with figures

422 POWDER FLASK, of engraved steel and wood ; and one, of engraved brass and steel

423 FLASK, enamelled with Diana and Actæon and Cupid, mounted with silver gilt

424 POWDER FLASK, and spanner combined, of steel; and a spanner and powder measure combined

425 TWO SPANNERS; a powder flask, with leather pouch; and a primer

426 STEEL POWDER FLASK, with chased brass lions' heads; powder horn, with spanner; and a powder horn—*found at Bridlington*

427 THREE MODELS OF PISTOLS; and knife, of brass and steel

428 LOBSTER-TAILED HELMET—*temp. Charles I.*
 From Alton Towers

429 HEAULME OF SIR W. BIFORD, it is remarkable for having a defensive demi-mentonnière with the original crest, the coronet is of later date

430 HEAULME—*temp. Maximilian*
 From Battle Abbey Church

431 HELMET, with crest attached, said to be that of Sir Anthony Brown
 From Battle Abbey Church

432 JAMBE, of plate mail; and long-toed solleret, with spur—*early 15th century*

433 JAMBE AND SOLLERET—*temp. Edward IV.*

434 SOLLERET, with spur attached, and gauntlet with gadlings at the knuckles—*15th century*

435 PLAIN CHAMFRON—*temp. Maximilian*

436 BUCKLER, with hook to attach it to the girdle—*temp. Maximilian*

437 CIRCULAR SHIELD, engraved with heads and ornaments—*Italian*

438 PLACCATE, ornamented with coronets and plumes, the letter F and double triangles, originally plated with silver—*Spanish*

439 BASCINET—*temp. Edward VI.*

440 TILTING HELMET, with jointed visor and demi-mentonnière
 From Aylesbury Church

441 PIG-FACED BASCINET—*very rare*
 From the Castle of Herr von Hulshoff, Bavaria

442 STEEL SADDLE-BACK, with a combat of warriors in repoussé work, inlaid with gold and silver—*16th century*

443 PLACCATE, with tasset attached—*temp. Maximilian*

444 SHIELD, of steel, chased with Mars and Venus in the centre, and wreath border

445 CABASSET, engraved with ornaments—*temp. Queen Elizabeth*

446 MORION, with comb, finely engraved and chased—*temp. Queen Elizabeth*

447 MORION, of polygonal form—*temp. Queen Elizabeth*

448 SALADE, bearing the armourer's marks, with movable visor—*temp. Henry VII.*

449 MORION, with three combs—*temp. Elizabeth*

450 BREASTPLATE AND PLACCATE, engraved with bands of ornaments with slot for lance rest—*temp. Queen Elizabeth*

451 SALADE, of classic form—*temp. Edward IV.*

452 MORION, with high comb, engraved with arms and scroll ornaments divided by plain bands—*temp. Elizabeth*

453 CABASSET, with bands of engraved ornaments and medallions—*temp. Elizabeth*

454 SADDLE, covered with plates of steel—*15th century*

455 SADDLE-TREE, covered with gesso duro, modelled in low relief, with numerous figures in the costume of the 15th century and bound with brass—*temp. Edward IV.*

456 SADDLE, the flaps of embroidered leather, the whole bound with bone—*end of 15th century*

457 RUSSET AND GOLD MORION, with ear-pieces, engraved with the arms of Saxony, figures in medallions, and bands of ornaments, studded with lions' heads, the plume-holder formed as an arabesque figure—*temp. Phillip and Mary*

458 GRANDE GARDE AND MENTONNIÈRE, a pièce de renfort for tilting—*temp. Edward IV.*

459 RUSSET PAULDRON, with chased brass fleurs-de-lys and suns, the cognisance of Louis XIV.

460 PLACCATE, for the back, of fine Italian workmanship, with damascened borders, in centre a band with compartments formed of raised silver studs, and a repoussé medallion of a female leaning on a column

 Engraved in Fairholt's 'Miscellanea Graphica,' p. xix. fig. 2

461 CASQUE, with plume-holder, triple ridge and support for plume embossed with ornaments and fleurs-de-lys, part of the armour of an officer of the guard of Cosmo de Medici

462 PAIR OF GAUNTLETS, of russet steel and gold, with bands of ornaments and the device of Henry VIII.: a full-blown rose and true lover's knot

> *From Lord Pembroke's Collection*
> *The rest of the suit is at Windsor Castle*

463 PAIR OF STEEL MITTEN GAUNTLETS, divided in the centre, and with fluted ridges across the knuckles, engraved with bands of ornaments

464 FLUTED BURGONET, with visor formed as a human face with moustache—*very rare*

465 WAISTCOAT CUIRASS, engraved with bands of arabesque figures and military trophies—*temp. Henry II. of France*, VERY RARE

466 CUIRASS, with tassels, engraved with a combat of naked figures, bands of ornaments, the Crucifixion, and a knight kneeling, armourer's marks—*German, temp. Henry VIII.*

467 TROOPER'S BOOT

> *From the battle-field of Naseby*

468 CANNONS, a pair, of bronze, richly embellished with hunting trophies, &c., and the arms of Nassau, inscribed " Johannes Burgheruys me fecit 1678 "

469 CANNONS, a pair, one has a shield of arms, and the other is dated 1636

470 CHAMBER OF AN IRON CANNON—*found at Passage, West Cork ;* and a cannon, ancient Irish make—6 *ft. long, found in a bog at Bandon, Co. Cork*

471 Two GUNS, of brass—captured in the Redan, by Col. MacMahon, bearing the emblems of Venice, an inscription in Russian punched on the breech

End of Third Day's Sale.

Fourth Day's Sale.

On MONDAY, JULY 9, 1888,

ORIENTAL ARMS AND ARMOUR.

480 Two CUTTARS, inlaid with gold

481 CUTTAR, the blade with equestrian figures in relief, the handle inlaid with gold; and one, with silvered and gilt hilt, the sheath silver mounted

482 CUTTAR, the hilt inlaid with gold; and two others, of plain steel

483 PAIR OF CHINESE SWORDS, brass mounts with carved wood grips; and two pairs smaller; and one made of coins

484 THREE KREESES, two with silver wire grips

485 KREESE, with silver-mounted sheath; and one, with carved ivory handle

486 FIVE KREESES, with wood handles

487 YATAGHAN, with ivory handle; and one, with broad blade

488 CHURAH, the blade and hilt damascened with gold, it belonged to Gholat Singh; and a Ghoorka knife, the blade inlaid with gold, and with velvet sheath, with two small knives, mounted with gold filigree

489 FIVE GHOORKA KNIVES

490 MORESQUE DAGGER, with fish-skin grip, chiselled steel pommel, the sheath mounted with chased and pierced silver

491 PERSIAN DAGGER, and a Turkish dagger, with chased silver hilt and sheaths

492 CINGALESE SWORD, silver hilt, with animals' heads, the scabbard mounted with chased silver ; and a dagger, with silver-mounted sheath, the hilt terminating in a bird's head

493 DAGGER, with ivory hilt and silver-gilt sheath; and one, with silver-gilt hilt and scabbard

494 DAGGER, with chiselled steel blade, inlaid with gold and silver mounted hilt

495 CINGALESE DAGGER, with carved handle mounted with chased silver, the scabbard cased with silver ; and a smaller dagger, with carved ivory handle

496 DAGGER, with bloodstone handle, the sheath mounted with chased silver, the blade of chiselled steel inlaid with gold

Presented by Count d'Orsay

497 CINGALESE DAGGER, in silver sheath ; and a smaller ditto

498 DAGGER, with broad channelled blade inlaid with an inscription and ornaments in gold; and one, with ivory hilt and silver-mounted scabbard

499 DAGGER, with broad blade, the hilt of ivory, carved with figures and animals

500 FOUR ABYSSINIAN DAGGERS ; one, with broad blade ; a Chinese knife ; one in tortoiseshell case ; and a wooden dagger

501 DAGGER, with steel hilt and pierced pommel; a knife, with ivory handle ; and two others

502 ELEPHANT GOAD, with inlaid ivory handle ; and a Chowry handle, cased with silver, engraved and partly gilt

503 KNIFE, with ivory handle carved with figures ; one, with pierced and carved handle ; and one, with ivory handle

504 KNIFE, with enamelled handle terminating in a grotesque head ; and a silver-mounted scabbard

505 DAGGER, with green-stone handle, silver-mounted sheath with turquoise ; a dagger, with agate hilt ; and a knife, with jade handle

506 AFGHAN KNIFE, with long blade and lacquered handle ; kreese, with engraved blade and agate handle ; a small Yataghan ; and a knife, with pierced steel handle

507 DAGGER, the blade with Oriental inscription, and with ivory and amber handle ; and a Burmese knife, with ivory handle carved with figures

508 DAGGER, with blade inlaid with silver, the hilt and sheath studded with coloured stones

509 DAGGER, with curved blade mounted with chased silver, in silver sheath ; and a dagger, with long blade inlaid with gold, the hilt and scabbard silver mounted

510 DAGGER, with long blade inlaid with inscription in gold, chased silver hilt and sheath

511 SWORD, with channelled blade, nielloed silver hilt, and mounts to sheath

512 Two MAHRATTA SWORDS, with chased and gilt gauntlets

513 SCIMITAR, with silver hilt and mounts to scabbard ; and one, with ivory hilt

514 INDIAN SWORD, with straight blade ; one, with waved blade ; and a scimitar, with chased hilt

515 SCIMITAR, the blade with ridged back and inscription in gold ; an Indian sabre, with grooved blade and steel hilt ; and a scimitar, with brass hilt

516 Two SPEARS, the staves mounted with chased silver

517 EXECUTIONER'S AXE ; and one, with long bamboo handle and silver rattle

518 FIVE SABRES ; and two Chinese swords

519 EXECUTIONER'S SWORD, from Borneo ; one, with carved horn hilt ; one, with Damascus blade ; Chinese sword, with long handle ; and two others

520 Two INDIAN AXES ; one, with head inlaid with gold ; the other, chased and partly gilt

521 MACE, with hand guard ; and one, with wooden handle

522 AXE, with chased head ; and a battle hammer, the head cased with silver

523 Two CHINESE DOUBLE SWORDS, in scabbards; and two others

524 SEVEN CHINESE AND JAPANESE SWORDS

525 SWORD, with curved blade, channelled and inlaid with gold, the sheath mounted with engraved silver gilt

526 SWORD, with short broad blade, the sheath mounted with silver; and scimitar, with blade inlaid with a long inscription in gold, chased metal sheath

527 THREE PERSIAN DARTS, tipped with silver, in silver-mounted sheath

528 SCIMITAR, with chased and channelled blade, inlaid with inscription in gold, the blade divided in two near the point; and an Indian scimitar, with engraved and silvered hilt

529 INDIAN SCIMITAR, with heavy blade, the hilt chiselled and engraved with flowers; and one, the blade inlaid with gold

530 SWORD, with straight channelled blade, engraved and gilt hilt; and one, with serrated blade, divided at the point, engraved with inscription

531 SCIMITAR, with blade of chased steel, inlaid with inscription in gold, and chased silver guard

532 EXECUTIONER's SWORD, with broad blade, strengthened and mounted with chiselled steel; and a sword, with chiselled hilt

533 SCIMITAR, with blade inlaid with gold, fish-skin scabbard, mounted with nielloed silver

From the Collection of Prince Potemkin

534 SCIMITAR, the blade inlaid with an inscription in gold, in silver sheath, with figures and ornaments of niello work

535 SCIMITAR, with blade engraved with an inscription, horn handle, and silver-mounted sheath

536 SCIMITAR, with silver-mounted scabbard; and a scimitar, with blade inlaid with gold, and black horn handle

537 KNIFE, with long blade inlaid with gold, with ivory handle; and one, smaller

538 YATAGHAN, mounted in chased silver, the hilt of horn, the sheath silver mounted—*taken at Seringapatam*

539 YATAGHAN, with blade engraved with inscription, walrus handle, silver mounted and inlaid with coral

540 YATAGHAN, mounted with silver, the sheath with chased metal mounting

541 AXE, with stone head and short handle, of chased metal gilt; a scimitar blade, inlaid with gold; and an Eastern dagger, with silvered guard forming a gun rest

542 SHORT BATTLE-AXE; an axe, with pointed blade; and an elephant goad, the head partly chased

543 FOUR MACES

544 FIVE BATTLE-AXES

545 SCIMITAR, the blade inlaid with inscriptions in gold, the hilt engraved and gilt, and velvet belt, with nielloed silver ornaments, formerly belonging to Tippo Sahib; and a scimitar, with scabbard, given by Mahomed Ali to Lt.-Col. Carodoc, at Cairo, 1827

546 ALBANIAN PISTOL, with flint-lock, the stock mounted with chased silver; and a double-barrel pistol, with flint-locks inlaid with gold, the butt terminating in a poniard

547 Two PISTOLS, with locks mounted with nielloed silver

548 PAIR OF FLINT-LOCK PISTOLS, mounted with chased silver

549 Two PERSIAN PRIMING FLASKS, of metal enamelled in colours

550 FLASK, of horn and ivory, silver mounted and inlaid with gold; and one, with chased silver filigree set with coral

551 ALBANIAN FLINT-LOCK GUN, the stock covered with silver and inlaid with coral

552 Two MATCH-LOCK GUNS, the butts and stocks mounted with chased and engraved brass

553 GUN, with match-lock, the stock inlaid with mother-o'-pearl and metal work; and one, with chased metal mounts, flint-lock and stock inlaid with brass work

554 GUN, with square barrel, damascened raised work with inscription and Hindoo deities

From Warren Hastings' Collection

555 INDIAN GUN, with match-lock, barrel inlaid with gold and lacquered; and one, with steel butt and chased barrel

556 SIEGE GUN, with long barrel and match-lock—*Chinese*

557 CHINESE MATCH-LOCK

558 CIRCULAR SHIELD, of hide, with ornaments in gold; and four gilt bosses; and a large powder horn, covered with leather

559 PAIR OF ARM-GUARDS, of steel, chased with ornaments in relief

560 ARM-GUARD, of chiselled steel inlaid with gold; and a pair of Moorish stirrups

561 SHIELD, with broad border of ornaments inlaid in gold; and four perforated and gilt bosses

562 SKIRT OF STEEL MAIL, with engraved plates; and a helmet

563 HELMET AND SKIRT OF CHAIN MAIL

564 TURKISH HELMET, of chain mail, and steel plates and armlet to match

565 TARGET, with match-lock pistol in the centre, and an aperture above for taking aim

From the Tower

566 SHIELD, of rhinoceros horn, with bosses

567 Two SHIELDS, with brass bosses

568 CUIRASS, in five hinged pieces, richly inlaid with gold ornaments and inscriptions

569 CUIRASS, in four pieces, with inlaid gold borders

570 SUIT OF ARMOUR: consisting of helmet of chiselled steel, with flowers and trellis pattern, the border inlaid with gold, chain camail, cuirass formed of four plates, and two arm-pieces

571 HELMET, with camail and nasal guard inlaid with inscriptions and ornaments of gold

572 HELMET, fluted and engraved with scroll work, with nasal guard and neck guard

573 HELMET, with chain camail, plume-holders, inlaid with inscription in gold

574 HELMET, with camail with coins attached, plume-holders, nasal guard inlaid with inscriptions and ornaments in gold

575 THREE COATS OF CHAIN MAIL

576 SHIELD, of steel, richly damascened and inlaid with small turquoises and rubies (three bosses missing)

577 INDIAN SHIELD, of buffalo hide

SUITE OF CARVED AND GILT IVORY FURNITURE.

Presented to Warren Hastings by Tippo Sahib.

578 An Armchair
579 A Ditto
580 A Ditto
581 A Ditto
582 A Sofa
583 A Small Table
584 A Ditto
585 A Card-table

WEAPONS USED BY SAVAGE TRIBES, Etc.

586 Six Assegais; and eleven spears
587 Large Wicker Shield; a stone axe-head; three arrows; a chowry; a boomerang
588 A Bow; a quiver, with arrows; nine South Sea clubs; and an axe
589 A War Club; and fourteen other South Sea weapons
590 Two Swivel Guns—*from Amoy*
591 Coat of Leather—*from Patagonia*
592 A Caffre Shield, of painted wood, inlaid with shells; and a small shield, of rhinoceros hide
593 Six Indian Spears
594 An Arab Spear; three lances; and one, with very long bamboo staff
595 A two-handed Chinese sword; and an executioner's sword
596 Four Bundles of Spears
597 A Narwhal Horn—*about 6 feet long*
598 An Elephant's Tusk
599 A Paddle; an African spear; a pacha's horse tail, with staff; and a staff, with feathers

600 A STAFF, of hippopotamos hide; a blowing stick; and ten spears and assegais

601 A CHINESE HELMET; a flag; and a pair of stirrups

602 Two SMALL CANNON-BALLS, connected by five sharped edged bands of steel; a dagger; and four knives

603 BORDERERS' KNIFE; Highland dirk; a Bowie knife; two others; and three axes

604 A SILVER-MOUNTED PHILIBEG; a horn; and a silver buckle

605 CAP, of a Carlist general; a Russian cap; and a horn walking-stick

606 CATALAN KNIFE, with inscription on blade; one other; two small daggers; and two pocket-knives

607 Two SPOONS; two Maté cups; one silver mounted; two tubes; and a musical instrument

608 FOUR NORTH AMERICAN INDIAN ROBES; and a hat

609 STEEL Bow, inlaid with silver; one, of rhinoceros horn; and three bundles of arrows

610 Two QUIVERS; arrows; a tomahawk; a rhinoceros-horn whip; a Tartar whip; an opium pipe; and a hand-jingle

611 A LARGE TIKKI, of green jade

612 A DITTO

613 Two BRIDLES; and two lassos

614 Two CARVED CHINESE BAMBOO MATCHPOTS

615 BETEL-NUT CUTTER, inlaid with silver; and a smaller ditto

616 TURKISH HANGING-LANTERN, of perforated metal, with enamel bosses

617 TURKISH BRIDLE, ornamented with silver; crupper; and pad

618 SADDLE; pair of chased silver stirrups; crupper; and silver-mounted and embroidered saddle cloth
From Monte Video

619 SADDLE AND HARNESS, of embossed leather
From Buenos Ayres

620 SIX BRACKETS, composed of pistols

621 FOUR DITTO

622 Two FLAGS, carried by General Lord Howden at the funerals of George IV. and William IV.

623 Two TUSKS; and a candle, from the wreck of the Royal George

---

624 VARIOUS STONE SPEAR-HEADS; bronze Celts; arrow heads; &c.— thirty-six pieces

625 SEVEN CIRCULAR ENGRAVED SLABS, of white stone; and a ring

624A PAIR OF SILVER FILIGREE EARRINGS; a necklace of monkeys teeth; and an embroidered apron

624B ELEPHANT'S TUSK, used as a war triumph in India

626 A ROMAN BRONZE STIRRUP—*found in Cannon Street*

627 A SPEAR-HEAD—*found in the Thames;* nine others; and an iron axe-head

628 NINETEEN BOLTS, for crossbows

629 EIGHT LOCKS; a spanner; and six padlocks

630 NINE EARLY BRITISH SWORDS AND DAGGERS; a lance-head; and two other pieces—in a glazed case

631 ROMAN BOW BRACER; two bronze spurs; a bronze buckle

632 NINE INSCRIBED LEADEN BULLETS—*from Marathon;* two bronze bowls; and a small figure

633 FOUR BRONZE SPEAR-HEADS; and a sword

634 ETRUSCAN BRONZE HELMET, of classic form, with ear-pieces

635 GREEK BRONZE HELMET, brought by the late Lord Londesborough from Olympia

636 GREEK BRONZE HELMET
From Mr. Borel's Collection

End of Fourth Day's Sale.

Fifth Day's Sale.

———◦◦⚬⚬◦◦———

On TUESDAY, JULY 10, 1888,

AT ONE O'CLOCK PRECISELY.

———◦◦⚬⚬◦◦———

641 KNIFE AND FORK, with ivory handles, in nielloed silver sheath, with inscription and date 1707; and a knife and fork, inlaid with gold, the sheath of silver gilt, chased with an inscription and ornaments

642 TWO KNIVES, with inlaid ivory handles

643 CASE, for a knife, fork, and spoon, of cuir bouilli, silver mounted; and a smaller ditto, of tooled and gilt leather

644 CARVING KNIFE AND FORK, the handles of gilt steel and ivory, the blade partly gilt and engraved with a male and female figure, arabesques, and a cardinal's hat and arms—*17th century*

645 KNIFE, with broad blade, with Italian inscription, and brass-mounted handle; two Spanish knives, with openwork blades; and one, with carved ivory hilt

646 COUTEAU TRANCHANT, FOURCHETTE ET PAREPAIN, mounted with transparent amber handles, on the inner side of which are placed small medallions of figures, with ivory pommels in form of trefoils, and amber medallions inserted, the blades ornamented with damascened scrolls—*24½ in. long, 16th century*
   From the De Bruge Collection

E

647 KNIFE, with broad blade, partly engraved ; and a pair of knives, the handles of ivory, engraved with flowers and fruit, and green bands. The blades are engraved, the one with a grace before, the other after meat, with the music to which they were to be chanted

From the Bernal Collection

648 KNIFE, FORK, AND SPOON, with handles, formed of pieces of rock crystal, mounted with silver gilt

649 Knife and fork, handles carved in ivory, with grotesque masks and scrolls ; knife, fork, and pointed instrument, with carved ivory figures in costume of the 17th century ; and a small knife and fork, with ivory figure handles

650 Knife and fork, with horn handles carved in scrolls, and at the end of each the head and fore-legs of a goat ; and knife and fork, brass handles, champlevé enamels in blue and white, terminating in griffins' heads

651 A knife, fork, and spoon, of Venetian glass ; and clasp knife and fork, with steel handles, inlaid with cupids and animals in gold

652 KNIFE AND FORK, with ivory handles, carved with a stag and boar hunt

653 KNIFE AND FORK, with ivory figure handles ; and a knife, the handle formed as a man with a hurdy-gurdy

654 HUNTING KNIFE, the blade engraved with a stag hunt ; and one, the blades engraved with a crest

655 TROUSSE DE CHASSE, with eight implements, with engraved ivory handles

656 METAL-GILT FORK, on the top is a jointed figure holding a saw ; and a knife, with agate handle, mounted with silver

657 KNIFE AND FORK, with silver handles, minutely engraved with figures of Faith, Hope, and Charity ; knife and fork, with silver-gilt handles, ending in cherubs' heads ; and knife and fork, with mother-o'-pearl handles

658 CURIOUS WOODEN KNIFE, rudely carved, having on the blade a triangular opening, from the top of which hangs a small bell and a whistle on the handle, called the "Couteau Rodomont" or "Rodomont-Messer"—*there are printed German verses by Hans Sachs, the cobbler-poet of Nuremberg, on each side*

659 SILVER FORK AND SPOON, *Anglo-Saxon*. The spoon is formed of a flat piece of silver with oviform ends, one larger than the other, and a circular disc in the centre; on the front may be traced the usual interlaced pattern slightly engraved, with an ornament also on the disc; on one of the shanks may be seen the terminal animal's head, 8½ *in. long ;* the fork has an oval end with lozenge centre, and at the other extremity two prongs without any ornament, 7½ *in. long—found with some Saxon pennies of Coenwulf and Ethelstan, and other relics of the 9th century, at Sevington, N. Wilts, in* 1837 ; fork, 7¾ *in. long ;* and spoon, 8½ *in. long*

From Mr. Loscombe's Collection

660 SILVER-GILT SPOON, twisted handle, engraved at the back of the bowl, with broad bands of foliage, a crown and the letters I.R.; and one, with a square-shaped handle and rings attached

661 SMALL SILVER-GILT SPOON, shield-shaped bowl and twisted shank, at the end a male figure, holding on his head a pebble; and horn spoon, the handle carved with goats in relief, and silver-gilt border round the bowl

662 KNIFE, with mother-o'-pearl handle ending in a Corinthian capital, on which is a lion sejant, bearing a shield of a cross and crown, the same arms on the blade, in a carved boxwood sheath mounted in silver

From the Bernal Collection

663 POCKET-KNIFE, with steel handle, massively inlaid with gold, subjects the Virgin and Child, and a saint praying, with scrolls and arabesques; on the top are the letters AMR.PF.F.— 16*th century*. On the back of the handle is a case for another implement

From the De Bruge Collection

665 CASE OF TWELVE KNIVES, on the sides of the handles are placed plaques of transparent amber, beneath which are gilt representations on one side of saints, and on the other Scriptural sentences ; at the end knobs of the same material in form of vases, on the silver rim back and front is engraved " *Leonardus Marius,* 1634 "

666 STILETTO, with ebony handle, and sheath carved with dragons ; and a large pocket-knife, with three blades partly engraved and gilt, and with engraved ivory handle

667 SILVER FOLDING SPOON, with a fork attached through loops to the bowl, on the top a figure of Mars, on the slide which passes up the shank, a cupid, the interior of the bowl engraved with fruit —*16th century*

668 SILVER SPOON, the knob with flat end engraved with a pelican— *London hall mark,* 1589

669 SILVER-GILT SPOON, the handle and bowl enamelled purple, green, and white, with crescents and scrolls in slight relief

670 PAIR OF BOXWOOD SPOONS, the handles of silver gilt terminating in female busts ; and folding spoon, with shell bowl ; and silver shank and fork

671 IVORY SPOON, the handle carved with a female figure seated on an animal ; and a horn spoon, carved with a carriage
From the Bernal Collection

672 SILVER FOLDING FORK AND SPOON, with ivory handles inlaid with silver ; five spoons, with handles inlaid with coral and mother-o'-pearl ; and one, with ivory handle

673 SILVER SPOON, with chased spiral handle and engraved bowl ; and a parcel-gilt spoon, with ornaments and arms in niello

674 SILVER SPOON, parcel gilt, with German distich on the shank, at one end angels holding shields, the other a female bust

675 HUNTING KNIFE, in leather sheath, mounted with perforated steel, containing two smaller knives

676 HUNTING KNIFE AND FORK, with buckhorn handles carved with dogs and stags, in stamped metal case with coat-of-arms and figures dated 1592

677 HUNTING KNIFE, with partly engraved and gilt blade, buckhorn handle terminating in a Turk's head, the sheath containing a smaller knife with similar handle

678 ROSE AND CROWN, of wrought-iron work

679 WARDER's HORN, of bronze, inscribed "Petrus Gheyncus me fecit. Florint, 1466 "
From the Duc d'Abrantes' Collection

680 Two HERALD's STAVES, of painted wood, carved with coats-of-arms and animals

681 ARCHER's SHIELD, of ivory, engraved with St. Sebastian, arms, and flowers, inscribed Erasmus Arscot, 1680

682 RHINOCEROS-HORN STICK ; a cane, with chased steel top ; and two others

683 STAFF, with crook top and mounts of chased metal gilt

684 STAFF, with metal top, with the Royal arms; and a Spanish staff, with chased silver ball top

685 SMALL IVORY FLASK, carved with heads in medallions

686 EGYPTIAN GLASS LAMP, with perforated metal top

687 SMALL WOOD CASKET, with bands of steel terminating in acorns— *15th century*

688 BRONZE GIPCIÈRE, of oval form, with a loop and swivel at the top ; and one, with catch to attach to a belt

689 SMALL LEATHER JEWEL CASE, stamped in gold, with figures and ornaments

690 JEWEL BOX, covered with Gothic openwork steel

691 SMALLER DITTO

692 WOODEN BOX, with three carved panels, on the top; at the sides, nondescript birds and animals, with brass bands and lock—*15th century*

693 BAS-RELIEF executed on speckstein or hone stone, most elaborately
carved, representing the Crucifixion of our Saviour and the two
thieves; the principal figures in the foreground are in high
relief, the countenances full of expression, and the details of
arms and drapery highly finished; the piece was dedicated to
Michael Cranchfeld, of Erfurt, by Israel Vander Mullen, 1515
—10½ *in. square*

In an ebony frame, with engraved ivory border

694 THE MAGICAL SPECULUM OF DR. DEE, thus described in the
handwriting of Horace Walpole, which still remains at the
back of the case, signed H. W.: "The Black Stone into which
Dr. Dee used to call his spirits, *v.* his book; this stone was
mentioned in the catalogue of the collection of the Earls of
Peterborough, from whom it came to Lady Elizabeth Germaine
—H. W." The Black Stone, as it is called, is flat, and has a
highly polished surface, about half an inch in thickness, and
7¼ in. in diameter, perfectly circular, except at the top, where
a sort of loop is formed, in which is a hole for the purpose of
suspension

*It was purchased at the Strawberry Hill sale by Mr.
Smythe Pigott, and at the sale of Mr. Pigott's library in
December 1853, was bought for Lord Londesborough*

695 CRYSTAL BALL

696 REPRESENTATION IN COLOURED VENETIAN GLASS, of a group in
full relief of Diana and three nymphs surprised in a bath by
Actæon—in frame, on which are placed buttons set with
imitation gems of enamel—9½ *in.* by 7½ *in.*

697 CANDLESTICK, of iron, with spiral stem; and one, with spring stem

698 PORTION OF A PYX, bronze gilt, representing three soldiers,
watching the body of our Saviour

Found in the Temple Church, vide ' Gentleman's Magazine,'
1833

699 TWO METAL-GILT DOOR-HANDLES, formed as dogs

701 MINIATURE PISTOL, with spanner; a pair of miniature pistols and
bullet mould; a pair of miniature shears; and a small brass
steel yard

702 PAIR OF SMALL MODELS OF CANNONS; and a pair of small models
of mortars

703 PAIR OF BLUE STEEL SCISSORS, inlaid with silver; a stylus; and
a steel instrument

704 SURGICAL SAW, with chased and engraved frame, and handle of
ebony and ivory

705 BEAM AND INDEX, of a pair of scales; the beam is of steel, the
handle and hooks of engraved brass in openwork scrolls, hares,
hounds, and stags, with a ring at top, and bosses of animals'
heads

706 PAIR OF PERFORATED STEEL TONGS; a pair of screw nutcrackers;
and a sword-catch

707 SIX SILVER DICE, formed as figures of men in various attitudes

708 PAIR OF STEEL NUTCRACKERS, inlaid with gold, the cracker formed
of an animal's head opening its mouth; and a pair of pliers

709 DENTIST'S INSTRUMENT, with German inscription, and date 1508;
and a pair of steel pliers

710 TWO POMMELS, for swords, of steel, chased with figures in high
relief—*Italian*

711 SHEATH, for a knife and fork, of metal, chased with sacred subjects
in relief

712 BEGGING-BOX, of metal, triangular form, with figures of St. James,
St. Claude, and St. Lawrence upon the sides

713 CIRCULAR METAL ASTROLABE, with graduated index, the plate
engraved with signs of the Zodiac, days of the week, month,
year, &c., and a coat-of-arms with two bears as supporters—
$4\frac{1}{4}$ in. diam.

714 SQUARE SUNDIAL, with indexes, with gnomon and directions for its elevation, plummet level, &c., on the back is a movable Kalendar, made by Johann Martin, Augsburg, in leather case—$2\frac{1}{2}$ *in. square*

715 BARREL PADLOCK, the key on being pushed down the barrel forces out a grotesque mask at the bottom and releases the hasp

716 LOCK, from the principal gate at Hougomont
Presented by T. Crofton Croker, Esq.

717 ENGRAVED STEEL PADLOCK, the hasp with a brass dial to open when set at 6.20; and two keys

718 FETTER-LOCK, with key

719 BRASS-FRAME LOCK, with key and four brass knobs for turning the bolts, having on the outside two indices and dials with numbers the surface ornamented with brass scrolls on steel, the works, springs, and bolts being of steel, and brass hasp—17*th century*, 9 *in. long by* $4\frac{1}{2}$ *in.*

720 BRASS LOCK, with steel bolts and springs, the plate and the clamps for the bolts engraved, and on each side are three chased lions, the works enclosed in a brass box with key—17*th century*, $10\frac{1}{2}$ *in. by* 6 *in.*

721 STEEL LOCK, for a large coffer or *bahut*, with double clasp and beautifully worked key with an infinity of wards, the handle cut à jour, the surface of the lock ornamented with steel open scrolls —16*th century*, 7 *in. by* 4 *in.*

722 LOUIS XV. SPEARHEAD, inlaid with dogs and ornaments in gold; a smaller ditto; and an oval steel box, chased with a portrait, surrounded by arabesques, the bottom engraved with the Judgment of Paris—*inscription, and date* 1694

723 STEEL MIRROR, the back with Moorish ornaments and with spirally fluted handle

724 Two SMALL RUSSIAN TRIPTYCHS, of enamelled brass

725 SILVER DITTO, with figures in relief, the ground filled with black enamel

726 LEADEN PLATE, supposed to have been a book-cover with three holes at the side, in one of which is still a ring with an inscription in Anglo-Saxon, found in the grounds of the Abbey of Bury St. Edmunds, Suffolk. At the head is a Runic inscription, stating it was the Book of Ælfric

The translation by Mr. Wright is given in 'Miscellanea Graphica' (page 12), as well as a woodcut of this unique example—6½ in. by 5 in.

727 SILVER CASE, engraved outside with personifications of the twelve months and constellations, containing a pair of compasses, rule, and pencils—3½ *in. long*

728 SILVER CASE, engraved outside with astrological signs, &c., containing dice and a teetotum for games of chance—3½ *in. long*

729 SILVER CASE, engraved outside with zodiacal signs for astrological calculations, with an index at top, containing a rule, pair of compasses, square, pen, and point—3½ *in. long*

730 THIRTY DRAUGHTSMEN, of silver and silver gilt, chased with cupids and emblems, and with German inscriptions on the reverse

731 SILVER GIPCIÈRE, of triangular form, the border highly ornamented, chased with medallions of Mars and Minerva, masks and arabesques, on the top is a loop and swivel, and at the back are seen the holes through which the silk or leather of which the purse was made was attached—*Renaissance, 16th century*

732 EARLY VENETIAN FLASK, with a bird in high relief, the ground of brass inlaid with silver ornaments, and with movable handle

733 SMALL SILVER VASE-SHAPED INCENSE-BURNER, with chains

734 PENDANT, of silver gilt, with filigree centre to contain a relic, and short chased chain to attach to girdle

735 CARTOUCHE BOX, of silver gilt, chased with trophies of arms and vine border, with silver-mounted strap ; and two embroidered ditto

736 PAIR OF SILVER BADGES, partly gilt, with masks, trophies of arms and ornaments, with inscriptions and date 1720

737 GIRDLE, of silk, mounted with silver plaques and rosettes with Gothic buckle, terminating in a figure, and with a figure of a saint in niello in a niche—*14th century*

738 DANISH GIRDLE, of silver gilt, with two bosses in the centre, plaques with warriors' heads surrounded by scrolls

739 BUCKLE, of metal gilt, partly silvered, chased with figures, masks, and ornaments of openwork—15th *century*

740 GIRDLE, of enamelled metal gilt

741 DITTO

742 SWORD BELT, bandolier from the Imperial Armoury, Vienna; and leather patron

743 LEATHER QUIVER, containing bolts for a cross bow; and a windlass

744 MEASURE, for powder; and implement of torture

CARVINGS IN IVORY AND WOOD.

745 POWDER FLASK, of ivory, carved with a tiger hunt in relief, mounted with silver

746 STIRRUP, of wood, carved with a cherub's head
Said to have belonged to Montezuma

747 ELEVEN CHESSMEN, carved in walrus tusk, being two kings, three queens, three bishops, two warders (castles), and one knight, part of a large hoard of about 70 similar objects discovered in 1831 at Uig, Isle of Lewis, Hebrides
For a detailed account of their discovery, see ' Archæologia,' vol. xxiv. p. 212; Wilson's ' Prehistoric Annals of Scotland,' p. 567; and 'Miscellanea Graphica,' pl. viii.; the remainder are in the British Museum
From the style of ornamentation, they may be safely attributed to the 12th century, and are extremely rare

748 IVORY CHESSMAN, representing a bishop seated, the head and crosier broken off; in front are three smaller figures of saints, one pointing to a book, another holding a scroll, the centre figure playing on a harp; the sides of the chair are open and the back carved at top with three saints under canopies, and openwork foliage—13th *century*, 3 *in. high*

749 Draughtsman, of flat circular form, the device cut out from the surface, leaving a chevron border, and in the centre a centaur holding a club in his right hand, and lifting one of his hind legs with the other—13*th century*; bone draughtsman; and one other, of the 12*th century*

Found in a tumulus near Amiens

750 Fool's Bauble, or Jester's Staff, elaborately carved in boxwood; on the top is a lion seated on a pedestal of ten columns, holding in front a coat-of-arms surmounted by a cardinal's hat; beneath this is a large head with open mouth, and several other projections down the stem of a man playing the bagpipes, another seated, a bird, and several faces of men and animals; it is carved also in relief with Scriptural subjects, animals, and foliage, scale-pattern handle—27 *in. long*

From Cardinal York's Collection

751 Main de Justice, or Ivory Sceptre; on the top is a hand with the thumb and two first fingers extended in benediction, on the third, which is bent, is a gold ring set with a pearl, on the wrist is a ruffle; there are three convex bands inscribed in relief "Ludovic," "Rex," "Francorū"; two towards the top, and one, above the handle, also some raised leaf mouldings on the plain staff; the knob is decorated with fleurs-de-lys and leaves. Said to have belonged to Louis XII.—30 *in. long*

From the De Bruge Collection

752 Oviform Box, of ivory, straight-sided, with bands and lid of silver gilt; round the centre is carved in relief, on one side, a hunter blowing his horn, with stag and hounds, on the other, two grotesque animals with human heads, and between are three quatrefoil ornaments, originally inlaid with blue and red enamel —15*th century*

753 Circular Ivory Mirror Cover, divided by the stem of a tree in four compartments, in each of which are a male and female figure in attitudes of courtship, illustrating some one of the early Fabliaux—14*th century*, 3½ *in. diam.*

754 Circular Ivory Mirror Cover, representing the Assault of the Castle of Love; a knight on horseback, with a shield of three roses, is met at the gateway by two ladies armed with branches of flowers, another is shooting a rose from a bow, whilst others are scaling the walls by a ladder on one side and by a tree on the other, five females above are pelting them with roses; at four equidistant parts of the outer circle have been nondescript animals (two now wanting)—*14th century*
Bernal Collection

755 Circular Ivory Mirror Cover, within a tressure of eight arches is a tree dividing the relief into two compartments, representing a courtship and man kneeling crowned with a wreath by a lady —*14th century*

756 Circular Ivory Mirror Cover, of a gentleman and lady on horseback, and behind an attendant armed with a spear; at the four corners are leaf ornaments, forming a square (two now wanting)—*14th century*

757 Mirror Cover, with nondescript animals at the four corners; a gentleman and lady playing at chess on a small square table— *14th century, 3½ in. diam.*

758 Memento Mori, or Ivory Group; the principal figures are, on the one side, a youthful female figure holding a flower to her breast with coif and tresses, and on her feet the square-toed shoes of the 16th century; on the other, a skeleton, with worms crawling about (the jaw injured), round the pedestal, enclosed in a palisade and gates, are two allegorical groups of a youth drawing his sword, with a hound and tiger on either side, and a fool between an ape and a lion—*16th century, 11 in. high*

759 Large Ivory Male Figure, bare head, clothed to the knees, holding in one hand a globular cup, the other hand pointing to it; supposed Roman, but probably of a later period—*17 in. high*
From Mr. Webb's Sale

760 CONVEX CARVING IN IVORY. perhaps the front of a pax, representing the Virgin and Child with a Saint on each side; beneath is inscribed in Gothic characters, " Marya ; " above. a canopy and foliated border —15*th century*, 3½ *in.* by 3 *in.*

761 THREE IVORY DICE, of grotesque nude figures forming cubes, each facet being marked with dots, from 1 to 6—15*th century?*

762 IVORY DIPTYCH, representing eight subjects from the Life of Christ, under canopies of double trefoil arches of the Annunciation, Nativity, the Adoration, Entry into Jerusalem, Christ teaching in the Temple, the Betrayal, Last Supper, and Crucifixion—14*th century*, 9½ *in.* by 6¾ *in.*

763 IVORY DIPTYCH, in four subjects under trefoil arcades, the Nativity, the Adoration, Crucifixion, and Resurrection—14*th century*, 4½ *in.* by 5 *in. open*

764 IVORY TRIPTYCH, in the centre, Christ praying on the Mount, with foliage at the corners—*a carving of the* 16*th century*, 2¾ *in.* by 4¾ *in.*

765 IVORY DICE BOX, with coat-of-arms and crests of Brunswick in front—17*th century*, 3¾ *in. high*

766 SQUARE IVORY STEM, divided into twelve compartments of trefoil canopies, in each of which is a Saint—14*th century*, 6½ *in. long*

767 CARVED BONE BOX, of the 15th century ; on the top are Tom the Piper, Maid Marian, the Fool with his staff, Morris Dancers, coloured ; round the sides, Coursing, a Tournament, and Gathering Apples ; at the bottom is a chequered board for chess or drafts—7 *in.* by 5½ *in.*

768 ONE LEAF OF AN IVORY POCKET COMPASS AND SUN DIAL, carved with various devices in relief ; on one side, a dial with sunken space for a magnetic needle, a cardinal's arms and crests, and the sacred monograms ; on the other, a large round space for a movable calendar, at the bottom of which is a dead body and the mottos " Mors omnium finis " and " Virtus post funera crescit "—5 *in.* by 3 *in.*

769 IVORY POCKET COMPASS AND DIAL, of two leaves, with calendars and movable indices, engraved and painted, maker Leonard Miller, 1627—4 *in.* by 2½ *in.*

770 IVORY POCKET COMPASS AND DIAL, of two leaves, with calendar, movable index and German inscriptions, engraved, by Hans Ducher of Nuremberg—4 *in.* by 2½ *in.*

771 IVORY BATON, or Sceptre of the Electors of Germany; the stem is carved with twisted cords, stems and leaves, the handle with vine and grapes; the mace is hexagonal, with busts of the Emperor and five Electors at top and their coats-of-arms beneath, all of which are stuck on to the plaques—18*th century, 29 in. long*

From the Collection of M. Martenango of Wurtzburg

772 COFFRET DE MARIAGE, of hexagonal form, the lower part ornamented with slips of bone carved in subjects illustrative of some of the Fabliaux of the 14th century, at the angles are turrets dividing each subject, on the pyramidal cover is a border carved in ivory of angels and foliage, the framework is of marqueterie, with ivory and coloured woods disposed in patterns and borders —15*th century, Venetian, 12 in. high* by 11 *in. diam.*

From the De Bruge Collection

773 IVORY TANKARD, carved with the subject of the Triumph of Alexander over Darius, with numerous figures and borders at the top and bottom of martial and musical instruments; ivory terminal figure on the handle, and gilt-metal knob—6½ *in. high*

774 IVORY BUST OF A SATYR, with goat's horns, ears, and beard, on black pedestal—16*th century, 6 in. high*

775 IVORY EQUESTRIAN STATUETTE OF LOUIS XIII., in armour, beneath the horse is a tilting helmet, on a black pedestal—8½ *in. high*

776 GROTESQUE IVORY FIGURE, painted, representing a corpulent Spaniard, in black coat and silver buttons, on his head a night cap, his toes turned in, and bow-legged, holding out a small snuff-box the head takes off and forms a snuff-box, which can be taken out by a spoon attached to the other end of the hand, which is removable and enters at his side, on wooden pedestal with drawer—11 *in. high*

IVORY HUNTING HORNS.

777 BEAUTIFUL AND VERY RARE OLIPHANT, or Hunting Horn, of ivory; at the large extremity is a band 2 in. wide, beautifully sculptured in bas-relief with the legend of St. Hubert. The story is thus told :—The first compartment represents the chateau, at the portal of which are two females, one wearing a wimple and resting on a long stick, the other younger, holding two children by the hands—his mother, wife, and children taking leave of Hubert the hunter. 2nd. Hubert is seen mounted on his galloping steed, blowing his horn in all the excitement of the chase. 3rd. An attendant on foot pushing his way through the thicket, and two dogs worrying a stag, one of which is biting his haunches. 4th. Is the horse without his rider, feeding, his bridle hanging on a tree. The fifth represents the stag at bay, and from between its horns is seen a crowned head addressing the Saint, who is kneeling on one knee, with his hands raised, the horn hanging over his shoulder. In the last is the hind part of the horse, indicating his return to the chateau from which he started. The other end of the ivory terminates in a female head, the hair brought round the back of the head in two plaits. The silver mountings are a gilt embouchure and two bands, one at each end under the carvings, with trefoil ornament at bottom and engraved with animals ; from these is a transverse band running along the concave part of the horn, engraved with nondescript animals, and three shields of Arms of Bavaria, &c., with a buckler and ring by which to suspend it—*the work is of the beginning of the 15th century, 15 in. long by 3½ in. extreme width*

From the De Bruge Collection

778 SOLID PIECE OF RED CORAL, with three branches, on the ends of which are three whistles of different notes ; the rappel belonging to the same horn, and purchased with it—*2½ in. long by 1¾ in. wide*

779 LARGE IVORY WARDER'S HORN, rudely carved with four bands of imaginary monsters—many of which are identical with the engraved Gnostic gems—serpents, toads, the owl, cock, fish, birds, and other creatures. At the broad end is a band of hieroglyphics or magical signs, which are also placed between the carved animals, being scratched or cut on the surface; the smaller end represents a fish's head, from the jaws of which the mouth-piece protrudes. It appears to have been originally painted—perhaps of *Scandinavian* workmanship—28 *in. long*

780 IVORY HUNTING HORN, carved with interlaced circular medallions, in which are represented the wild boar, stag, fox, hare, squirrel, goat, and birds, and two oval of a deer and a bear. The embouchure is on the inner side, with a hole at the extremity to vary the tone, and a loop cut through the solid ivory for a strap. There are two silver bands with repoussé leaf ornaments and chevrons. It has become much discoloured, probably from being steeped in oil—*12th century*

781 IVORY WARDER'S HORN, very massive, with four carved bands of animals, real and imaginary. In the first is a man clothed in mail armour. It has two bronze bands and a chain; the mouth-piece is wanting. The work appears of the 12th century, and is said to have been the tenure horn of the Forest of Dean—21 *in. long*

782 IVORY WARDER'S HORN, the mouth-piece is formed of a human head; about the middle of the horn are engraved six coats-of-arms, one of which has been cut out and replaced by other bearings, immediately below are two bands of semicircles and squares. At the broad end is a carving in relief of a hunting scene, at the door of a chateau are a lady and attendant, two horsemen with horns, and three hounds chasing two stags, and two birds perched on one of the trees, and Gothic quatrefoil moulding—*14th century ;* the surface of the ivory has a sort of white coating, occasioned apparently by its long immersion in water, and is said to have been found in the Thames; at either end is a groove to pass a cord for suspension —22½ *in. long*

783 HUNTING HORN, of ivory, carved at the broad end with a border of lions and eagles in squares, the body has interlaced bands, in which are harpies, griffins, &c., and is bound with five silver belts engraved with running leaf pattern—*12th century*

784 IVORY HUNTING HORN, carved in low relief, with rude figures of two hunters and spears, dogs and ornaments, the costume appears to be that of the time of Edward I., but the interlaced ornament earlier, the mouthpiece is at the side—20 *in. long*
> *From the Bernal Collection*

785 IVORY HUNTING HORN, carved all over with scrolls, a mounted huntsman in costume of the 17th century, wild boar and hounds. There are two oval coats-of-arms surmounted by an imperial crown, and underneath the date 1763, the mouthpiece proceeds from a wolf's head—16½ *in. long*

786 IVORY HUNTING HORN, elaborately carved all over with trophies of hunting implements, wolf and dogs, coat-of-arms and bust of the Czar Peter of Russia

787 ANCIENT CHARTER HORN, made of the horn of the Highland buffalo (Buculæ cornu, or bugle horn), mounted in brass with hoofs, and long inscription by its former possessor, Mr. Baylis, of Prior's Bank, Fulham

788 CARVED BOXWOOD BOX, with the Sacrifice of Isaac on the top, and a man holding a jawbone before another man seated at bottom—*date* 1600

COMBS.

789 EARLY FRENCH BOXWOOD COMB, with large and small teeth, in the centre a carving of an allegorical subject, two cockatrices supporting a bell, underneath which is a dead fox and a cross, also two cocks on either side, animals and a man leading a bear, a distich in old French, " Prenez au gré ce petit don," &c., on the other side a rude carving representing the Virgin and Child and the Three Kings coming with presents—9 *in. long* by 7 *in.*

790 BOXWOOD COMB, with pierced geometrical and fenestral ornaments, inscribed " Je le donne pour bien "—8¾ *in.* by 8 *in.*

F

791 BOXWOOD COMB, with pierced geometrical ornaments and medallions of a stag and heart pierced by two arrows—8½ *in.* by 4½ *in.*

792 IVORY COMB, the centre band representing on one side a huntsman mounted with horn and hounds and attendants hunting the wild boar, on the other a font in which are two children with sponsors or gossips, and the fool, who is being attacked by the attendant with a squirt, a soldier on guard, and the father and mother ; a border at each end of vine leaves and grapes ; probably a christening gift—15*th century,* 6¼ *in.* by 5¼ *in.*

793 IVORY COMB, with one row of teeth, the band at the top carved in low relief, representing on one side courtship of three couples, one lover presenting a wreath, the second playing on a pipe, the third holding a bird ; on the other side is a marriage procession, the bride and bridegroom crowned with a wreath of roses, preceded by men playing the pipe and tabor, followed by three others—15*th century,* 5¾ *in.* by 3½ *in.*
From the Bernal Collection

794 IVORY COMB, with double row of teeth, a broad band divided into three compartments, on each side divided by columns supporting Gothic trefoil arcades of carvings in relief of subjects from the Life of Christ; Crucifixion, Entombment, and Resurrection, &c., with fenestral decorations at the corners—14*th century,* 5¾ *in.* by 4¾ *in.*

795 IVORY COMB, representing in relief on one side two ladies and gentlemen on horseback with hawks and hounds, on the other two horsemen and attendants hunting the stag; with scrolls at the corners—16*th century,* 7 *in.* by 5½ *in.*

796 IVORY COMB, of Oriental workmanship, carved à jour with scrolls, squirrels, and birds—6½ *in.* by 3 *in.*

797 IVORY COMB, of Oriental work, carved à jour with two deities seated on a couch and two birds, scroll borders top and bottom —4¼ *in.* by 5 *in.*

798 SMALL PLAIN BOXWOOD POCKET COMB, used by the American Indians

799 TRIANGULAR HORN COMB, with three rows of teeth, the centre carved à jour, and painted with two coats-of-arms and crests, at top the date 1723, and below the initials I.S.H. and R.E.H. in a wreath supported by two cupids, two square pieces of mother-o'-pearl inserted at the corners—6½ *in. diam.*

800 TORTOISESHELL COMB, engraved with large flowers, in a shell case, engraved with vase of flowers and pine-apples, inscribed "Jamaica 1683"—7 *in.* by 4½ *in.*

End of Fifth Day's Sale.

Sixth Day's Sale.

On WEDNESDAY, JULY 11, 1888,

AT ONE O'CLOCK PRECISELY.

ENGLISH SILVER COINS.

801 William I. Pennies, 3, Bonnet type, full face, and Sceptre and Pax ;
and William II., *scarce—fine*   4

802 Anglo-Gallic, Aleanore, Richard I., Henry II., and Hugo   9

803 Stephen, Eustace, Henry II., Richard, and John   10

804 Richard II., 3 ; Henry III., 4 ; Edward I. and Henry IV., &c.
    25

805 Edward II. and III., and Henry VI.   27

806 Edward IV., Richard III., Henry VII. and VIII.   19

807 Mary Groats, 2 ; Philip and Mary Shillings, 2 (1554 and one un-
dated), and a Groat—*all fine*   5

808 Edward VI.—Testoons 3, Shillings 2, and Sixpence 1   6

809 Elizabeth Hammered Money 13, and 3 Milled   16

810 James I. Shilling, Newark Ditto, and Charles I. Half-crown   3

811 Charles I. Oxford Twenty-shilling Piece, 1643—*fine*   1

812 Charles I., 6 Shillings and 8 small pieces   14

813 Charles II., small pieces 5 ; James II., 4 ; William and Mary, 4 ;
Anne, 3   16

814 George I., 6 ; George III., 19 ; William IV., 5 ; Victoria, 2   32

MEDALS.

815 *Silver.—Ob.* Bust of Van Tromp in high relief, *Rev.* Ships in action

816 —— Charles II.—*Ob.* Bust, *Rev.* Institutor Augustus, 1673

817 Large Silver Medal of George IV.—*Ob.* Bust, *Rev.* Trident, Greek inscription—*by Pistrucci*

818 *Silver.*—George II. and Queen Caroline—*Ob.* Their Busts, *Rev.* Busts of seven children, 1732

819 —— Charles I., satyrical, struck at Leyden—*Ob.* Bust, *Rev.* A hydra and Dutch inscription; and a small medal of Charles, Prince of Wales   2

820 Bronze Medal of Mary I.—*Ob.* Bust, *Rev.* " *Cecis Visus Timidis Quies* "; and another, gilt, of Admiral Van Tromp   2

821 Bronze Series of Napoleon Medals, in two cases

822 Silver Medallet of Charles I., in a chased border, by Rawlings, with loop

ROMAN IMPERIAL DENARII.

823 Julius Cæsar—*Ob.* Bust, *Rev.* Sepullius Macer, Venus standing; Augustus—*Rev.* S.P.Q.R. in a buckler; Nero—*Rev.* Emperor standing; Otho—*Rev.* " Securitas "—*all fine*   4

824 Cleopatra—*Ob.* Her Bust, *Rev.* Bare Head of Antony, Antoni Armenia Devicta—*rare and fine*   1

825 Tiberius—*Rev.* Emperor seated—*very fine and rare;* Claudius—*Rev.* Prætorian Camp—*also fine*   2

826 Vespasian, 2—*Rev.* Female seated, holding palm branch and standard, *Rev.* Female Bust, " Paci Orb Terr Aug": *Rev.* A sow and three piglets—*scarce and fine*   3

827 Domitilla—*Ob.* Bust, *Rev.* Fortune standing—*very rare and fine*   1

828 Domitian, 8—various reverses; and Titus—*Rev.* Quadriga—*all fine*
9

829 Trajan, 4—*Rev.* Fortune, *Rev.* Mars, *Rev.* "Alim Ital," *Rev.*
"Dac Cap"; Hadrian, 5—*all well preserved* 9

830 Plotina—*Ob.* Her Bust, *Rev.* Bust of Trajan—*extra fine and rare*
1

831 Antoninus Pius, 2; Faustina, 1; Aurelius, 3; Sept. Severus, 4
—*all well preserved* 10

832 Clodius Albinus—*Rev.* Hands joined, holding a standard—*rare;*
Antoninus Pius, 1—*Rev.* Bonus-eventus holding a patera;
Aurelius, 2; Faustina, sen., 1—*all fine* 5

833 Julia Domna, 3; Caracalla, 4; Plautilla, 1; Geta, 3—*all fine* 11

834 Macrinus, 3; Diadumenianus, 1; Elagabalus, 4; and Cornelia
Paula, 1—*well preserved* 9

835 Aquillia Severa—*Rev.* Concordia—*very fine and scarce;* Sœmias,
1; Maesa, 1; Sev., Alexander, 3 6

836 Barbia Orbiana—*Rev.* Concord seated—*scarce and fine;* Mamæa,
3; Maximinus, 1; and Paulina—*Ob.* Bust, *Rev.* Empress on
a peacock—*very rare and fine* 6

837 Trajanus Decius, 2; Etruscilla, 2; Etruscus, 1; Hostilianus, 2;
Treb Gallus, 3; Volusian, 3 13

838 Mariniana, 2—*Rev.* Consecratio—*scarce;* Æmilianus, 1; Valeri-
anus, 3; Saloninus, 1; Salonina, 2 9

839 Gallienus, 7; Postumus, 11; Claudius Gothicus, 2; Marius—
Rev. Felicitas; Maximinus Daza—*Rev.* Quadriga 22

840 *Silver.*—Constantine the Great—*Rev.* Virtus Militum, the Prætorian Gate with the doors thrown open—*extremely fine* 1

841 —— Johannes—*Rev.* Urbs Roma, Rome seated; Theodosius—
Rev. Wreath; Arcadius; Gratianus; Victor; Julianus; and
Valens—*all well preserved* 7

842 Silver Quinarii—Aelia Flacilla; Diocletianus; Justinianus;
Valentinianus; and three Greek coins 7

COINS RELATING TO BRITAIN.

CARAUSIUS.

843 *Silver.—Ob.* Bust, *Rev.* ADVENTUS AUG, The Emperor on horseback trampling on an enemy, a fulmen in the exergue—*very rare and in fine preservation*

884 —— *Ob.* Bust, *Rev.* EXPECTATE VENI, Emperor and female joining hands—*very rare and fine*

845 —— *Ob.* Bust, *Rev.* VOTO PUBLICO, and tablet inscribed MULTIS XX IMP—*rare and well preserved*

THIRD BRASS.

846 *Ob.* Portrait, *Rev.* VOTUM PUBLIC, Multis xx Imp, on a basket ; *Rev.* PROVID AUG, Providence standing; *Rev.* SECURITAS, Security leaning on a column ; *Rev.* MONETA AUG, Goddess holding cornucopia and scales—*all scarce and fine*   4

847 *Ob.* Portrait, *Rev.* Equitas Mundi, Goddess with scales and cornucopia ; *Rev.* PROVIDENTIA AUGGG, Goddess standing; *Rev.* PAX AUG, Female with lance; *Rev.* LAETITIA AUG ; *Rev.* MARS ULTOR ; *Rev.* FORTUNA—*all fine*   6

848 *Ob.* Fine portraits, *Rev.* VIRTUS AUG, Emperor with spear and shield ; *Rev.* FORTUNA, with wheel and cornucopia ; *Rev.* SALUS AUG, HYGEIA—*all very fine*   3

849 *Ob.* Bust of Emperor, in helmet, cuirass and shield, *Rev.* PAX AUG ; *Rev.* SALUS AUG—*both fine ; Rev.* Pax Aug, S.P. in field ; *Rev.* IOVI CONSERV, Jupiter standing ; *Rev.* Victory marching —*well preserved*   5

850 *Ob.* Busts, *Rev.* LEG IIII, a lion ; *Rev.* LEG VIII, a Bull standing ; *Rev.* A Ram ; *Rev.* PAX AUG, all with M.L. (Moneta Londinensis) in exergue—*well preserved*   4

851 *Ob.* Busts, *Rev.* FORTUNA ; *Rev.* PAX AUG ; *Rev.* Mars   5

ALLECTUS.

852 *Ob.* Bust, *Rev.* Iovi Conser, Jupiter standing; *Rev.* Pax Aug; *Rev.* Providentia; *Rev.* Virtus Aug, a galley; *Rev.* Fides Militum—*all fine*   5

853 *Ob.* Bust, *Rev.* Virtus Aug, a galley, 2—*both very fine*; *Rev.* Providentia; *Rev.* Pax Aug; *Rev.* Virtus Aug, Emperor standing; *Rev.* Hilaritas—*all well preserved*   6

854 *Ob.* Bust, *Rev.* Laetitia Aug; *Rev.* Pax Aug; *Rev.* Virtus Aug; *Rev.* A Galley, 3; *Rev.* Incuse Bust of Allectus   6

EARLY BRITISH OR GAULIC COPPER COINS, ETC.

855 *Ob.* Head, with curled hair, *Rev.* Rudimentary Horses, chariot, wheels, &c.; two, with the Minotaur; and three small coins, similar   6

856 Eight Gaulish Coins, with pressed obverses of heads, reverses of animals; and four others   12

857 Five curious inscribed Coins, cuno·to·rimo, m.a.; one, in silver, *Rev.* vlatos, a horse, *Ob.* Heads of Cupid   6

858 Eight Copper Coins, Gaulish, some Greek   8

859 Small well-made Mahogany Cabinet, for Roman Denarii

860 Two Small Cabinets, in form of books, bound in morocco, for Saxon and British Coins

861 Mahogany Coin Cabinets, brass bound, with Trays for English Silver

SAXON SKEATTÆ, STYCÆ, PENNIES, ETC.

863 *Ob.* Head—*Rev.* With Square Crosses and Animals   6

864 *Ob.* Without Head, various reverses, 7 ; and two coins of Sihtric

    9

865 Cunnetti ; Mirabilia ; Siefredus, 2 ; Burgred, 3—*Rev.* Guthere, *Rev.* Liafma, *Rev.* Dude Moneta   7

866 Eadbert, 2 ; Alchred, 2 ; Eanred, 4 ; Ethelred, 5 ; Osbrecht, 2 ; Vigmund, 2 ; Vulfhere ; Redulf ; and others   22

867 St. Eadmund—*Rev.* Cross ; Ethelbearht—*Rev.* Ethelere ; Egbearht —*Rev.* Bosel ; Ethelwulf—*Rev.* Ethelere ; Ethelred—*Rev.* Varin—*all fine*   5

868 Aelfred—*Rev.* Monogram of London, with portrait ; *Rev.* Cuthbert, 2 ; *Rev.* Redulf ; *Rev.* Dudig ; Cuthwulf   6

869 Aelfred—*Rev.* Eadwald ; *Rev.* Buga ; *Rev.* Diarmod ; Eadwig— *Rev.* Esculf—*scarce* ; Eadweard I.—*Rev.* Fulnad   5

870 Aethelstan—*Rev.* Athelvulf (Winchester) ; *Rev.* Wilebald ; *Rev.* Enberht ; Eadmund—*Rev.* Eadmund—*scarce*   4

871 Eadred—*Rev.* Theodmar ; Eadgar, 2—*Rev.* Fastolf ; *Rev.* Heinard ; Eadweard II., Bust—*Rev.* Elfvald Mo (Stanford) ; and two others—*some scarce*   6

872 Ethelred II.—*Rev.* Hand of Providence, 3 ; *Rev.* Long Cross, 3— *all fine*   6

873 St. Peter—*Ob.* A Sword ; *Rev.* A Temple ; Harthacnut, with portrait—*Rev.* Long Cross, Pulfren—*very rare and fine* ; Eadred—*Rev.* Landferth   3

874 Cnut—*Ob.* Bust, *Rev.* Cross and Moneyers, 4 ; Harold I.—*Ob.* Bust, *Rev.* Long Cross ; Harold II.—*Rev.* Cross and Moneyer   6

875 Edward the Confessor—*Ob.* Busts and King enthroned, various reverses   6

876 Carlus ; Ludovicus ; Margaret of Burgundy ; and five other pieces

    8

CELTIC ORNAMENTS.

877 PAIR OF SILVER ARMILLÆ, formed of plain wire, simply cut off at the ends—*found in Ireland ;* silver armilla, plain round wire, flattened out at the extremities—*found in Ireland ;* and Celtic bronze armilla, with broadish end, probably intended for an animal's head, and clasps

878 VERY LARGE SILVER PENANNULAR BROOCH, of solid metal, with a large arbutus or thistle ornament at each end, and another, which slides round the bar, to which was formerly attached the acus or pin (now wanting) ; these thistle ornaments are deeply cut in cross hatchings on the front, each point being a small annulet, the back flattened and decorated with a cross and a pellet in each angle—*found in 1853 on the banks of the Shannon, at Cloneen, Co. Longford, about 5 in. diam.*

879 PENANNULAR BROOCH, of gilt bronze, the edges are raised, and between the ridges are small square ornaments in relief ; the bottom of the fibula, or semicircular disc, has four bosses set with garnets in the centre, and three radiated bands, between which are scrolls ; the head of the acus is conical, with a large and small boss, each set with a garnet, and at the two upper angles are inserted pieces of lapis lazuli—*found in Ireland*

* The ornament at the top of the acus is so arranged as to be removed at pleasure, releasing it at the same time from the circular brooch.

880 SILVER PENANNULAR FIBULA, with broad flat ends, each ornamented with a double-corded border and six plain bosses, three of which only remain, the acus is quite plain—*found in Ireland ;* penannular fibula, with flattish bar and flat broad ends, each having five plain bosses, with interlaced ornaments between and corded border, the slide on the upper part of the acus is also ornamented—*found in Ireland ;* and silver penannular fibula, of a flattish bar and square ends, with raised lozenges in the centre, the head of the acus has the like ornament—*found near Tralee in* 1856

881 SMALL SILVER PENANNULAR FIBULA, the flat ends ornamented
with pellets in quincunx patterns—*found Co. Westmeath ;*
ancient Irish fibula, with long acus, the ends enamelled with
two red and black square ornaments, filled with green, the usual
animal's head at the junction of the ring; early Irish bronze
fibula, with animal's head and broad triangular ends, which have
been originally filled with enamel—*found in Waterford ;* bronze
pin, with ring end and a stylus—*found in Ireland ;* ancient
Irish fibula, the ends of which have been inlaid with enamel and
set with stones, now much corroded ; and oval leaden fibula,
with cross hatchings and five sunk holes for stones—*found at
Kilmainham, Ireland*

882 SMALL IRISH PENANNULAR FIBULA, with broad ends, inlaid with
enamel, portions of which remain, sufficient to ascertain its
original design ; the triangular ends were each ornamented with
a variegated bead in the middle, and three others round, two
at the broad end, the colours being a red centre, and blue and
yellow radiating lines, the interstices filled with white enamel,
at its juncture with the broad end is an animal's head ; it is
called the " Conyngham brooch "

883 THE " MOATE " FIBULA, with ring and long pin, the ends forming
a sort of trefoil scroll, with an interlaced knot, and set with two
garnets
Found at Moate, Co. Westmeath

884 EXTREMELY RARE EARLY IRISH SILVER PIN, or Acus Crinalis,
probably used for the hair, the lower part is plain, but ornamented towards the head in front with six square compartments,
the lower one ending in a point, in which are scrolls and other
devices, the interstices having been filled with enamel, traces of
which still remain ; the head or button, which projects at a right
angle, has also been enamelled, it is of fine work, and forms an
elegant head ornament—*12½ in. long*
Found in Ireland

885 PAIR OF MASSIVE BRONZE ARMILLÆ, with open ends, convex on the outer surface, engraved with chevrons, annulets, &c., and double-corded edge, patinated—*said to have been found in Ireland*; and Saxon silver bracelet, plain, with twisted ends fastened together, and two Saxon coins—*found in the Thames, near Deptford*

886 CIRCULAR BRASS BROOCH, formed of a broad band of metal engraved with four round compartments, in which are interlaced ornaments, and between leaves a rude animal, probably Scotch; and a Scotch circular brooch, similar to the last, with rude engraved ornament, and part of what appears to be an inscription, or perhaps the initials of the wearer

887 LATE ROMAN SILVER FIBULA, crescent-shaped at top, with pendant clasp, at the end of which is a button—*found in Cambridgeshire*; and bone hair-pin, the head in form of a cross, with an annulet in each arm, marked at the back with the Christian monogram $\frac{r}{x}$.—*found at the Cemetery, Aliscamp, Arles*

---

888 A LARGE BRONZE MEASURE, for grain, with two handles and three feet, with inscriptions and date 1670
From the Abbey Church at Selby

889 Two CAMP KETTLES—*found at Ampleforth*

890 AN ETRUSCAN BRONZE FIGURE OF A WARRIOR

891 A PERSIAN BRASS EWER; and dish, with strainer

892 A LARGE BRASS BOWL, engraved with characters

893 A DITTO; and two smaller ditto

894 A BRASS DISH, engraved and coloured; and a very large ditto

895 AN EGYPTIAN BRACELET, of coloured glass; one other; three bronze; and three bone hair-pins; and a pair of steel scissors

896 A JET SEAL; an amber bead, with early Irish inscription; and two others

897 IVORY ROULETTE BALL, with numerals, and engraved with animals ; a black ditto

898 THREE TRIANGULAR-SHAPED GOLD CLASPS, each set with three stones, two with garnets en cabochon, the other with pearls now decayed ; and a bronze ring, broken, fixed on a card

899 Two BRONZE TRUMPETS—*found at Killarney*

900 Two DITTO ; and one, of yew wood—*found at Diamond Hill, Killesandra*

901 A BRONZE AXE, terminating in a bird's head

902 VARIOUS STONE IMPLEMENTS—*found in Yorkshire*

903 VARIOUS STONE AND IRON CANNON BALLS

904 Six specimens of alabaster and antique marble, turned as balls

905 Sixteen smaller ditto

906 A marble bowl ; and a vase

907 Two alabaster slabs, carved with sacred subjects in relief ; and a blackwood slab, inlaid with a vase of flowers in mother-o'-pearl

908 A pair of sphynxes, of grey marble

909 A pair of Chinese paintings, of numerous figures—in blackwood frames

910 Two Chinese figures, carved in soapstone

911 Two bottles, of unglazed ware ; a small jar ; two coral snakes ; and deer's head

912 A Chinese bronze incense-burner, carved wood, cover and stand

913 A gong

914 A stone slab, carved with a landscape—in openwork wood frame

915 The Entombment, a relief in plaster, gilt—in blackwood frame ; and a wood slab, carved with a figure in a chariot

916 A crucifix, of wood, inlaid with engraved mother-o'-pearl

BRONZES.

917 Twelve circular medallions, of the Cæsars—in two frames

918 Four plaques, with subjects from Ovid in relief

919 Three ditto

920 Four ditto

921 Seven oval plaques, with classical subjects—in blackwood frames

922 An oblong plaque, with a panther and satyrs; and one, with infant bacchanals, after Flaxman

923 A pair of figures of children, emblematic of Music and Painting

924 An oblong plaque, with Europa; one, with two cupids and a lion; and one, with two horsemen from the Elgin frieze

925 A circular medallion of Alexander the Great; and three oblong plaques, with classical figures

926 A plaque, with Silenus in high relief; and one, with a Sacrifice

927 A circular plaque, with two figures of a female satyr and child; an oblong plaque, with a lion; and one, with a boar hunt

928 Four plaques, with figures of the Evangelists

929 A square plaque, with Christ and the Woman of Samaria; one, with the Last Supper

930 A circular plaque, with a saint; a gilt plaque, with the Madonna; and one, with two figures

931 A pair of medallions of Petrarch and Laura; and three others

932 An oval medallion of the Martyrdom of a Saint

933 Forty-eight bronze plaques and medallions, mounted on velvet

934 Twenty-three ditto

935 Twenty-nine ditto

936 Two circular medallions of horsemen; and a candlestick, on tripod, chased with foliage

937 A GROUP OF THREE ALLEGORICAL FIGURES—on marble plinth

938 THE DYING GLADIATOR

939 THE MARLI HORSES—*a pair*

940 A FAUN

941 A PAIR OF COPIES OF THE MEDICI VASE

942 TARQUIN AND LUCRETIA, a group in bronze—on marble plinth

943 HERCULES AND OMPHALE

944 THE LISTENING SLAVE

945 THE MERCURY OF G. DI BOLOGNA

946 THE APOLLO BELVEDERE—on marble pedestal

947 THE VENUS DE MEDICI

948 THE BORGHESE ATHLETE, by Zoffoli—on blackwood pedestal
    Signed
949 SATURN—on blackwood pedestal
950 CUPID SCATTERING FLOWERS—on bronze pedestal
951 AN ITALIAN BRONZE KNOCKER, formed as a female figure and two
    lions
952 A PAIR OF RECLINING FIGURES OF A RIVER GOD AND GODDESS
953 AN EQUESTRIAN STATUETTE OF THE DUKE OF WELLINGTON
954 THE MERCURY OF G. DI BOLOGNA—on marble pedestal
955 HERCULES AND OMPHALE, a pair of seated figures—on buhl pedestals
956 A GROUP OF A FEMALE FIGURE AND TWO CHILDREN

---

957 NAPOLEON'S CHAIRS, from the Island of Elba—*a pair*
958 Two footstools of carved and pierced wood
959 A glazed show-case
960 Two smaller ditto
961 Two ditto

MARBLE STATUES.

962 A NYMPH AT THE BATH, life-size marble statue, by
    R. J. Wyatt, of Rome—on marble pedestal
963 NARCISSUS, marble statuette—on scagliola pedestal
964 AMPHITRITE, marble statuette—on marble pedestal

SPORTING GUNS AND RIFLES.

965 A single match rifle, No. 515, by Whitworth—in case
966 A double ·450 bore deer-stalking rifle, No. 6984, by Purdey—in
    case
967 A single match rifle, No. C 926, by Whitworth—in case
968 A double ·450 deer-stalking rifle, No. 6948, by Purdey—in case
969 A similar rifle, No. 6949

970 A pair of double guns, 14 bore, Nos. 1837, 8, by Moore and Grey—in case

971 A single match rifle, No. 946 C, by Gibbs, of Bristol—in case

972 A double gun, 10 bore, No. 1211, by Moore and Grey

973 A single rook rifle, 380 bore, by Beattie

974 A double rifle, No. 3348, by C. Lancaster—in case

975 A single American match rifle, by James—in case

976 A single match rifle, No. 6415, by Purdey—in case

977 A double ·450 deer-stalking rifle, No. 5311, by Purdey—in case

FINIS.

London: Printed by Wm. Clowes & Sons, Limited, Stamford Street and Charing Cross.

www.ingramcontent.com/pod-product-compliance
Lightning Source LLC
Chambersburg PA
CBHW030000030726
47499CB00008B/2832